THE CURVE BALL

INDIANAPOLIS LIGHTNING SERIES BOOK 2

SAMANTHA LIND

SAMANTHALIND.COM

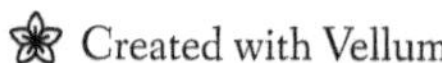 Created with Vellum

CONTENTS

ONE
JUSTIN

I stare in the mirror as I slide my snapback on my head. My game is on point tonight, and I'm looking forward to the attention it's going to bring my way. I have not had sex in a week, and that's the longest I like to go without it. It never takes me long to find a willing woman; fuck, some nights I can bring home more than one, making the night even better. Our opening day win earlier tonight will sweeten the celebrating I am about to do.

I grab my phone from the kitchen counter, hitting the home button to see if I've missed anything. A few missed calls from an unknown number is all I find. I slip my phone into my front pocket and my wallet into my back one as I grab my keys and head for the garage. I hit the button on the wall, opening the large double door just as my doorbell rings. *What the hell?* I am not expecting anyone, so I step outside from the open garage to see who might be here at eight pm.

"Hello?" I call out. I take in the piece of shit car parked

in my driveway and the woman who's standing at my front door. "Can I help you?"

"JJ, I'm sorry to just show up like this, but I can't do this anymore. I didn't have anywhere else to bring her. I've put formula, diapers, and a few changes of clothes in the diaper bag," she rambles on, and it is then I notice a baby carrier with a baby in it next to her feet.

"Excuse me?" I stammer as I realize the woman standing in front of me is Erica. We hooked up a couple of times last year. "What the fuck is going on here, Erica?" I demand.

"JJ," she sighs, like I should know what the fuck is going on. "This is Evelyn. She's yours. I'm sorry I never told you about her before now. I was trying hard to do this on my own, but I just can't anymore. Everything you need, including my cell number is in her bag," she tells me. "I'm sorry, but I've got to go," she says as she takes off for her car. I watch in complete shock as she runs for her car and peels out of my driveway, leaving the baby and diaper bag on my doorstep.

My attention is pulled from the empty road to the sounds of the baby crying on my doorstep. I don't know the first thing about babies. I'm only around them when I'm at my best friend and teammate, Derek's place. I fish my phone from my pocket, juggling it in my haste to get it out to call him for help. The baby is getting pissed as the seconds tick by. I wander over to her, picking the seat and bag up, and carry them into my house before I attract the attention of my neighbors.

"This better be important," Derek barks into the phone.

"It's an emergency, dude. I don't know what the fuck to do," I ramble into the phone.

"Slow down, what's going on?" He pauses. "Where are you?" he asks.

"Fuck, man. I am freaking out. A chick I hooked up with last year just showed up on my doorstep with a baby in hand and said I was her dad. Said she couldn't raise the baby and then fucking left. What the hell am I going to do? I know jack shit about babies, and how do I even know if she's telling the truth?"

"Holy shit. JJ, calm down. I'm on my way," Jillian, Derek's wife, says into the phone. I am obviously on speaker now, so she's heard everything I just said.

"Dude, what the fuck," Derek says. "Just hold tight, one of us will be over in a few," he says before the line goes dead.

I pace the living room as I wait for Jillian or Derek to arrive. The baby is still crying from her seat across the room, where I set it down. I don't even know how to take her out of the contraption, hold her properly, or get her to stop crying. *Fuck.* My mind starts to race as I try and figure out why Erica would do this and what the fuck I'm supposed to do with an infant.

I see headlights flash just as I hear the engine of Derek's truck turn off in my driveway. He lives in the same gated community as I do, which reminds me, I'll need to call up to the security gate tomorrow and find out how the fuck Erica got past it and to my house.

"What took you so long to get here?" I ask as Derek opens his truck door.

"I called Riley to come stay with the girls, but then we decided she would come with me rather than Jillian," he says as they both get out of the truck.

I lead us into the house. "I have no idea what the fuck to do. Help!"

"First off, calm the fuck down, dude. Babies feed off your stress," Derek states. We both watch Derek's sister, Riley, as she hurries over to the car seat and pulls Evelyn from it.

As soon as she cradles Evelyn in her arms, she immediately starts to calm down.

"What's her name?" Riley asks.

"Um, Evelyn is what Erica told me."

"Hi, Evie," Riley coos at the baby, and she stops crying almost immediately.

"Holy shit, you're the baby whisper," I state, amazed that she was able to calm her down so quickly.

"Not really," she says. "Did her mother leave you with anything? Bottles? Formula? Diapers? Clothes?"

"She left that bag." I point at the diaper bag sitting on the coffee table. "What the fuck am I supposed to do with a baby?" I ask the room at large. "I don't even know how old she is."

"If I had to guess, she looks to be about three months old," Derek says.

We watch as Riley walks over to the bag and rummages through it. She pulls out a bottle and can of formula and walks to the kitchen, which is off the living room. She comes back a few minutes later with a bottle made and the baby sucking hungrily at it.

"Looks like she was hungry," Riley tells us as she takes a seat on the loveseat.

"So, do you have any information on the mother?" Derek asks a few moments later.

"Um, some," I tell him. I pull my hat off and run my fingers through my hair, before replacing it back on my head. "Her name is Erica. We hooked up last year. She left me her cell number but said that she just couldn't do this on her own anymore and that it was my turn."

"That's pretty fucked up," Derek murmurs. "I think, tomorrow, you need to call your attorney and get the ball rolling on a paternity test. Maybe try tracking down this Erica chick and finding out as much as you can about the baby."

"What am I going to do with her when I go to practice? Games? Road trips?" I ask, freaking out again.

"Well, if Erica is truly out of the picture, you're going to have to hire a nanny."

"I can help," Riley interjects. "I haven't found a job yet, so I'm available if you need someone to watch her."

"There you go. Problem solved, for now," Derek says. "There isn't anyone Jillian and I trust with our kids more than Riley. She's the perfect person to help you until you can figure shit out."

"Thanks," I say, blowing out a huge breath. "I still can't believe that Erica just dumped the baby here and left. Who would do that kind of thing?"

"I don't know, but maybe it's for the best," Derek states.

"Do you have a guest bedroom?" Riley asks.

"Yeah, let me show you where it is." I lead her down the

hall, Derek grabs the diaper bag and follows behind, as well. I'm guessing we'll need whatever is in that bag for the night, so it's a good thing he grabbed it. I show Riley into my guest room, and she takes a seat on the chair in the corner as Evelyn continues to suck greedily on the bottle. I watch as Evelyn finishes it and Riley pulls it from her mouth. Riley turns her in her arms, laying her up on her shoulder, and starts patting her back. I have seen Jillian and Derek do the same thing with their girls, so it isn't completely foreign to me.

"Can you look in the bag and see if there's a burp rag or cloth, please?" Riley asks. Derek starts rummaging in there and pulls something out, handing it to Riley. She tucks it between her and the baby just seconds before Evelyn lets out a huge belch, followed by some spit-up.

"Are you sure you're okay staying and helping out tonight?" I hear Derek ask Riley as I step out of the room and into the bathroom in search of another towel to give her.

"Yeah, I'll be fine. Justin obviously knows shit about babies, so it's not like we can leave him alone with her. I'll call you in the morning. I only saw the one can of formula and a few diapers, so we're going to need to run to the store in the morning," I hear Riley tell Derek, and her assumption about me not knowing shit about babies is spot on.

"I'll get Jillian on it in the morning. Text her a picture of the formula so that she can get the same kind, as well as the diapers," Derek tells her as I run back down the hall to grab the car seat.

"Do you want this for her?" I ask, holding up the seat.

"It isn't recommended to allow babies to sleep in their

seats, but put it down over there, so I have it if I need it. I will just be careful and have her sleep next to me. Tomorrow, we can get a pack-n-play or crib for her to sleep in," Riley says as she lays Evelyn down on the bed. She must have moved over to it while I was out of the room.

"I'm so fucked," I say under my breath, "I don't know what I'd do if it weren't for you guys."

"We'll get you through this," Derek says, slapping my back. "I'm going to get out of here. Call me if you need anything. I'll keep my phone on and next to me all night."

"Thanks," I say, the stress starting to roll off me.

"We'll be fine," Riley calls out, calm as can be.

TWO

RILEY

"Do you need anything?" Justin asks once my brother has left.

"I'm good. I'll just get her changed and then try and get some sleep. She looks pretty tired, so I'm sure she'll sleep for the next few hours, at least."

"Okay. Thank you again for coming to my rescue. I owe you."

"It's not a problem, and my offer is still on the table to help you out if you need it. I haven't found a job, and I love working with kids," I tell him once again.

"Thanks, we can talk more about that tomorrow. Right now, my head is still just spinning over the events of the last hour. I still can't get over the fact that Erica just dropped her off and left. Who'd do that?"

"I don't know the details, but maybe she was having issues with postpartum depression, and this was her way of making sure that Evelyn was taken care of and not hurt," I suggest.

"Postpartum, what?" JJ asks, a confused look on his face.

"Postpartum depression. Many women suffer from it. With all the hormonal changes that happen after giving birth, it can mess with some women, so in the long run, it might have been for both her health and Evelyn's safety."

"Wow. I've never heard about it, but that doesn't mean much," JJ tells me. I sit back and observe him. It looks like he was dressed to go out tonight. I've only spent a little bit of time around him, mostly at Derek and Jillian's house or when I went with Jillian and the girls to training camp earlier this year. I can tell he's so out of his element, and I find myself biting back a laugh from escaping.

"I'm fine here if you want to head to bed. I'm going to myself right after I use the bathroom," I finally tell him. I make sure Evelyn is sleeping and in the middle of the bed. I grab two of the pillows and place one on either side of her. I don't think she'll go anywhere for the little bit of time I'll be in the bathroom.

"Is she okay there alone?" JJ asks as I step away from the bed.

"She should be. She's still pretty little to be rolling on her own. If you'd feel more comfortable staying with her while I use the bathroom, you can watch over her. I'll just be a minute or so."

I step into the connected bathroom and shut the door behind me. I lean against the door and draw in a deep breath, slowly exhaling as I rid the stress of the evening from my body. Tonight's events were a curveball, one that I'd never have seen coming.

I quickly use the bathroom then wash my hands, drying

them on the towel hanging from the holder. I pull the pony-tail holder off, shaking out my long blond hair and massaging my scalp. I slip the elastic band around my wrist as I flip the light off and open the door. Since I was already in yoga pants and a T-shirt when Derek called, I'm perfectly comfortable to slip into bed.

Once out of the bathroom, I take in the scene before me. JJ is watching Evelyn as she peacefully sleeps in the center of the large king-size bed. Her little hums are the only sound filling the room. I forgot how much noise that babies make while they're fast asleep sometimes. I've nannied for a few families over the years, plus helped out my brother and sister-in-law as I could when my nieces were babies. I spent a few weeks with them since I was still in school and could only spend some of my breaks with them over the last couple of years. I know they've had a rough year, but I am so glad that they found their way back to each other. My brother has changed so much, and all for the better from what I can tell.

"She's a good baby so far," I whisper, not wanting to wake her. I stop next to JJ at the edge of the bed.

"I'll take your word for it," he tells me before he turns and leaves the room. I pull the blankets back and place the two pillows on the far side of the bed. Once I've situated myself under the covers, I move Evelyn in next to me. Once we're both settled, sleep finally claims me.

THREE
JUSTIN

JJ: Dude, your wife and sister are lifesavers. I don't know how I'm ever going to repay them. Your wife showed up here with an SUV full of so much baby stuff it looks like a fucking Target exploded in my house.

Derek: Like I said last night, we're here for you, man. Let them help you. They know what they're doing. Just don't get any fucking ideas about my sister. I will kill you if you touch her.

JJ: I don't think I'll be touching another woman for a long fucking time at this point.

Derek: Don't say I didn't warn you. I know how you operate when you let the head below your belt do the thinking.

JJ: Point taken. Now back to WTF am I going to do?! I'm not cut out to be someone's dad.

Derek: Take a deep breath and deal with it, man. Have you called your lawyer?

JJ: Yes, he's going to send over a lab company to swab for paternity. Said that the test takes a couple of days to get the results. If it comes back positive, he'll file the petition with the courts for temporary full custody. I gave him Erica's information she left with me. Riley also found Evelyn's birth certificate and some other documents in the diaper bag, so we have that information as well. According to that, she's three months old like you thought last night.

Derek: Sounds like you've got things under control then.

JJ: If you say so.

Derek: Have you held her yet?

JJ: They made me just a little bit ago. After Jillian got here, she changed her into a new outfit and then handed her over to me for a little bit. I felt like I was going to break her. Riley also taught me how to change her diaper this morning. That was an event in and of itself.

Derek: I felt the same way when Addison was born. But you'll get used to it. Just take one day at a time. And welcome to diaper duty. There will be days you wonder how something so vile can come out of something so cute.

JJ: I called Coach and told him what was going on. I told him I might need a couple of personal days. He told me to keep him informed.

Derek: Are you going to go to practice this afternoon? I'm sure, between Riley and Jillian, they'll be more than happy to keep Evelyn for you.

JJ: I probably should. It would probably do me good to hit the gym and some balls today.

Derek: I'll see you there.

I place my phone onto the nightstand and head for the shower. After tossing and turning all night, I was up bright and early this morning to get a call in to my lawyer and another to Coach.

With things in motion on the paternity front, I can't dwell on the unknown, just move forward and deal with everything as we get more answers.

With my shower done, I pull on a team T-shirt and some basketball shorts.

"I was going to head into practice if you don't mind

staying here by yourself?" I ask Riley as I walk into the living room where she's on the couch. She looks a little tired this morning. I overheard her telling Jillian that Evelyn was up every three hours last night, hungry. That stopped me in my tracks. How often does a baby need to eat? How am I ever going to do this without someone's help? Fuck, I might need to call my mom to come to stay with me for a while.

"We're good here. I think little miss will enjoy some time in the swing while I grab a quick shower," Riley replies.

"Do you need help moving anything?" I ask, looking around again at everything Jillian brought over. I wasn't lying when I told Derek earlier that it looks like the baby department from Target exploded in my living room. Between the giant boxes from the swing, stroller, and pack-n-play, to the piles of clothes, diapers, wipes, bottles, and formula, this baby has taken over my house in the span of a few hours.

"I'm good. Do you have a room that you want me to set up as a nursery? I can move all of this into it and get it out of the living room." She asks, pointing to the assembled pack-n-play and swing.

"Umm..." I stammer. "I hadn't thought that far ahead. I guess we can make the room next to the one that you slept in last night the nursery. Did Jillian get everything that I'll need for a nursery?"

"She didn't get a crib or changing table, but the pack-n-play will work for both for now. Once you get everything figured out with the paternity and custody, you can go buy furniture."

"Okay. If you think of anything else I might need in the meantime, here's my credit card, you can go pick it up or order it online and have it delivered," I tell her, pulling one of my cards from my wallet and handing it over. I don't take Riley for someone that would run out and run a balance up with random shit, so I feel comfortable handing over my card and giving her free rein with it.

"Thanks," she says, a small smile pulling at the edges of her lips. My eyes lock on those lips, and I have to shake my head to stop the thoughts from forming of them wrapped around my cock. "Hey, do you think you could give me a ride over to Derek's before you leave? My car is at his house."

"Sure, I'm ready when you are."

"Let me just go grab the diaper bag and make sure it is packed, and then we can head out. Do you think you can put Evelyn in the car seat?" she asks.

"Ummm..." I hesitate, "I guess I can try. You might have to show me how the buckle works."

"That I can do. Give it a few days, and you'll be a pro at it," she says, flashing me a full-fledged smile.

I warily pick Evelyn up, making sure to support her neck like both Jillian and Riley showed me. I place her in the car seat and pull the straps over her shoulders. That's where I stop. The buckle is weird, and I have no fucking clue how to use it. I take the time to look at Evelyn. I take in her little button nose, her wispy, baby-soft dark blond hair. I don't miss the fact that it's the same color as my own. I don't think that she doesn't look like me, but I also don't think she does. But what do I know, I've never paid that close attention to what babies look like or who they resemble. I've only really been around a few teammates' kids, Derek's specifically.

"Did you get it figured out?" Riley asks, pulling my attention back to the present.

"Nope," I tell her, shaking my head side to side.

"It is not that hard," she says as she pushes me out of the way. She grabs both parts of the buckle and crosses them over each other. "All you have to do is just cross these two over each other, line them up with this and secure them into the bottom part." We hear the buckle click as she shows me how to do it. "And to unbuckle, you just press this button and pull up on these, and they'll come out. Give it a try," she suggests, since she's now undone the latch.

I grab both straps and fumble with aligning the two parts correctly.

"You've got it, just straighten them slightly, and you'll be okay." I do as she says, and sure enough, they fit together like they should and easily slide into the latch. "Now that you know how to work the latch, you need to learn about the straps. The chest clip should always line up with her armpits, and you should be able to pinch the straps and not have any slack. It isn't safe for there to be a lot of room between her and the straps. If you don't have them tight enough and you were in an accident, she could slide out of the seat. She also has to be facing backward for a while. It's safest for babies, even toddlers."

I look at her with a confused look filling my face. "Come again?" I say, dumbfounded.

"Don't worry, we'll get you all up to speed." Riley pulls

on a strap hanging from the bottom of the seat. It tightens down the straps holding Evelyn into the seat.

"That isn't too tight on her?" I ask.

"Nope," Riley says. "You want it tight enough that she isn't going to slip out in an accident, but not so tight she can't breathe. As long as when you attempt to pinch the strap at her shoulder and your fingers slip off and don't pinch extra strap, you know it's tight enough."

"Okay, are you ready?" I ask, not in any position to question what she has to say about anything to do with Evelyn.

"Yep, let's go." She tosses the strap of the diaper bag over her shoulder. I lift the car seat and follow Riley out to my car.

"So, how does this go in here?" I ask, opening the back door of my car.

"The middle is the safest place, so let's put it there. I'll see if I can find you a base for this type of seat. That will make getting it in and out much easier. You won't have to deal with the seat belt each time." I watch as she places the seat in and expertly straps it in for now.

"Thanks. I don't know what I'd be doing if it wasn't for you helping me out," I tell her as I back out of the driveway.

"I'm happy to help. I love kids, and Evelyn is such a good baby."

"I'll take your word for it," I tell her as I slip on my sunglasses. I roll down the street, keeping my speed on the lower end since so many people are outside playing in the beautiful weather that we're having lately. Springtime in Indianapolis can be hit-or-miss, depending on the year, and this one has been no different. Warm one day and freezing-ass cold the next.

We make it the few blocks over to Derek and Jillian's house. I kill the engine after parking in front of the extra garage bay door.

I step out of the car and watch as Riley gets the car seat out of the back. She flings the diaper bag over her shoulder and the seat in the crook of her arm. It is evident that Riley has done this many times and looks like a pro doing so. "Can I help with anything?" I offer before she gets too far ahead of me.

"I'm good," she says as she pushes open the door leading us into Derek's garage, and then into their house.

"Hey! How's it going?" Jillian asks as we enter the kitchen.

"Good. I had JJ bring me by on his way to practice so that I could grab my car," Riley answers her.

"How's this sweet little thing doing?" Jillian asks as she takes the car seat from Riley.

"She's been an angel," Riley states. I watch as Jillian sets the seat down and unclips the buckle, loosening the straps so that she can easily remove Evelyn from the seat. I know she's got two kids of her own, but she makes it look so simple.

"I'm going to head out, is Derek still here?" I state.

"You just missed him. He left maybe five minutes ago," Jillian tells me as she glances at the clock.

"Okay, I'll see you guys later. Should I come back here to pick her up, or will you go back to my place?" I ask.

"I guess that more depends on how long you're going to be gone," Riley states.

"A few hours. I'm not sure," I tell her honestly.

"Crap, I can't go back to your place, I don't have a way to get in."

"If you want to go back before I'm home, you can get in through the garage. The code is 2426."

"Okay, thanks," she says, flashing me a small smile.

"Bye, ladies," I say to Jillian and Riley, and I guess Evelyn, too, before I head back out the door.

Once in my car, I pull out of the driveway and onto the road. I exit the gated community a couple of minutes later and make a mental note, once again, to check in with them when I return to find out how Erica got in last night. I still can't believe that it was last night. On the one hand, it feels like it just happened, and on the other, it feels like that was so long ago.

I quickly make it to the clubhouse where I find a few of the guys already in the locker room getting ready to workout. Derek is in talking to one of the pitching coaches, so I stroll over to my locker and drop my keys and phone on the shelf, then sit down on the seat and change into my workout clothes.

"You ready?" I ask, stepping into the doorway of the office Derek is in.

"Just a minute," he says. I leave him to finish up his conversation and make my way down the hall and into the weight room. I find Matt O'Riley and Jose Martinez, a first baseman and outfielder, respectively, already working out.

"Hey, man," Matt calls out as he spots Jose as he lifts.

"Morning," I call out as I grab a set of dumbbells and find a spot to start my reps.

"Heard you had quite the night," Jose calls out once he's finished his set.

"Yeah," I grunt out between sets. "You can say that."

"So, what's the deal?" Matt asks as he switches with Jose.

"Don't know yet. We're going to do the paternity test later today. It takes a few days to get back. Once we have that, then my attorney can petition the courts for custody. At this point, I don't think Erica will challenge it since she did drop the baby off at my doorstep and take off."

"That's fucked up, man," Jose says.

"You're telling me."

"Do you believe her?" Matt asks.

"I don't know what I believe. Erica's timeline works out," I answer before starting another rep.

We fall into silence, only our grunts from lifting heavy weights fill the room. Derek finally joins us about fifteen minutes into my thirty-minute workout.

"How's Evie doing this morning?" Derek asks once we've finished up our workouts and are toweling off. I suck down half a bottle of Gatorade before answering him.

"Fine, as far as I know. Riley kept her most of the time. She didn't say that anything was wrong. I did hear her mention to Jillian that she was up every few hours feeding her. Is that normal?" I ask, dumbfounded.

"Yep. Babies have small stomachs, they have to eat every two, three, sometimes four hours. The older they get, the larger their stomachs get, and the more they can eat in one sitting."

"I'm so fucked," I tell him, wiping the sweat from my forehead and neck. I never planned to have kids. I was perfectly happy with my bachelor's life, so to say this was a curveball, that'd be an understatement.

"You'll figure it all out eventually," Derek assures me.

FOUR
RILEY

"So, how was your night?" Jillian asks as she snuggles Evelyn.

"It was fine. She was up a few times to eat and to be changed, but nothing out of the ordinary."

"She's just so sweet," Jillian muses as she sticks her nose into the crook of Evie's neck and breathes in her fresh baby smell.

"She sure is. It makes me have baby fever," I tell my sister-in-law.

"It's a good thing I'm already knocked up, otherwise, I'd be jumping Derek when he gets home after snuggling this one today."

"Ugh, I didn't need to hear that," I teasingly groan.

"Oh, please. Like you wouldn't jump JJ if the opportunity presented itself?" she asks, cocking an eyebrow at me.

I instantly feel the blush heat my cheeks. "Ummm..." I pause, thinking of how to answer her question. I've never had a conversation like this with Jillian, and it is not one I want to have right now. "No?" I finally say, but it comes out more like a question.

"I've told Derek a few times that I think the two of you would make the best couple. He's never been a fan of that idea, got pissed off at me for it once," she says as we move from the kitchen to the living room where the girls are playing and watching something on Disney+.

"I don't think I'm his type," I tell her honestly.

"I don't think that boy knows what his type is," she says, laughing. "But, I also think that when he finds a woman that has potential, he'll change his ways to be with her."

"Why's that?" I ask. I don't know a ton about JJ, but what I've figured out from the amount his name and picture gets posted in the media, and what Derek has mentioned over the years, paints him as the classic sports star playboy. The guy that jumps from model to actress to whatever next beautiful woman is waiting to hang off his arm.

"He's never been in a relationship since we've known him, or at least one that he's told any of us about. He likes to party and be unattached. So, as I said, I don't think he even knows what his type is."

I scrunch my nose up at her confirmation of my suspicion that he's nothing more than a playboy. "Yeah, no thanks. I have no desire to be the girlfriend at home while he's out being flashy and cheating on me."

"Has he said anything about you helping him with Evie until he can get things figured out?"

"We're supposed to talk about it more today. I told him I hadn't found a job yet, so if he wanted to hire me as a full-time nanny, I am available."

"That would be perfect for you!" she tells me, flashing me a huge smile. "Think of all the time we could spend together with the kids. Penn and Addy would love having you and Evie around all the time."

"That would be fun," I agree with her just as Evie starts to wake up and squirm in her arms. She lets out the cutest baby cries. I reach for the diaper bag and pull out a diaper and the wipes just as Jillian lays her down on the couch. She snags a receiving blanket from the top of the bag to slide under Evie before she unzips her sleeper and starts changing her diaper. While she does this, I grab the bottle I packed in the bag and add the formula to it, shaking it up so that it is ready for her once she's all put back together. "Want me to take her?" I offer once Jillian zips the sleeper back up and coos at Evie.

"I can." She picks Evie back up and cradles her against her chest as she reaches out for the bottle. I hand it over and watch as she offers it to Evie, who immediately accepts it and starts sucking it down greedily.

"Mommy, can I hold the baby?" my oldest niece Addison asks as she stands in front of Jillian.

"Maybe in a little bit. Evie's eating right now."

"Okay, Mommy," she says, and then climbs onto the couch between us.

"Come here, munchkin, Auntie needs some snuggles," I say as I reach for her. She starts to giggle before my fingers even graze her skin as I tickle her side.

"Auntie," she belly laughs. "Don't tickle me if you want snuggles." She finally gets out, and I stop and pull her into my lap.

"How's my favorite five-year-old?" I ask as I push some of her curls from her face.

"I'm not five yet," she dramatically tells me.

"You're not?" I playfully question her.

"Not until next month," she reminds me as if I didn't know when her birthday is.

"Ohhh," I exaggerate. "Are you going to have a party?" I ask, even though I already know all the details.

"Yes!" she practically yells right in my face due to her excitement. "A big party!"

"Awesome, think I can come?" I ask her, squeezing her in a hug as I do.

"Of course, Auntie Ry. You're my favorite," she tells me with a smacking kiss to my cheek.

"You're my favorite," I tell her, kissing her on the cheek in return. "What do you want for your birthday?" I ask, keeping this conversation going as Jillian stops to burp Evie.

"A pink bike and helmet, a sparkly dress, a new baby doll, and clothes, um..." She stops to think, tapping her cheek with a finger as she does so.

"Wow, those are some pretty cool things," I tell her.

"Auntie Ry, is that your baby?" she asks out of the blue as we watch Jillian cuddle with a now very relaxed and full Evie.

"Nope. That's JJ's baby. I'm just helping him watch her while he's at work."

"Uncle JJ's?" she asks, the question and disbelief evident in her voice. "No, Uncle JJ doesn't have a baby," she states matter-of-factly.

"Yep, she's his. He just found out about her last night."

"Wow," she says as her eyes get big. "Mommy, can I hold her now?" Addison asks again.

"Sure, you can, bug. Sit back on Auntie Ry's lap," Jillian instructs, and she does just as she's told.

"Look at you, such a big girl. You're going to be all trained and ready for when the baby comes," I tell her as she supports Evie's head correctly. I've got my hands on either side of her, just in case she needs someone to swoop in and help her support Evie's weight.

"When can I play with her?" she asks, smiling at Evie, who's starting to squirm around just a bit.

"Not for a few more months. Evie's still pretty little and can't play much," I explain. "It will be the same way when your baby sister or brother comes home. He or she will be small and fragile for a while. You'll have to be super careful and help Mommy whenever you can," I tell her quietly as I shift Evie in Addison's arms, taking most of the weight off of her, so she can touch Evie's face and grip one of her tiny fingers.

"Who's dis?" Penelope asks, joining us as she stands in front of us.

"That's baby, Evelyn," Jillian tells her as she scoots forward and picks Penelope up and sets her on the couch between us. Penelope looks over the baby and up at me, obviously very curious where this baby came from. "Uncle JJ is Evelyn's dad," Jillian explains to Penelope. She has almost the same look her sister had only a few minutes ago when she found out the same news.

"Okay," she says, leaning forward to place a kiss on

Evie's forehead before she slides off the couch and goes back to her toys and watching her movie.

"Oh, to be three and not have a care in the world." Jillian laughs as we watch Penny go back to playing.

"Did you think of anything that JJ might need for this cutie that I didn't bring over this morning?"

"Nope. I got the pack-n-play and swing all set up after you left. I'm sure we'll need to buy some more formula before the week is over, but that's easy enough to grab. He did give me his credit card and said to buy whatever she needed, so if I think of anything, I can either order it or go pick it up. I might see if I can find another base for the car seat. Either for my car or whoever he ends up hiring to watch her."

"That's a good idea. So much easier to just snap in than fumbling with the seat belt every time," Jillian confirms.

"That's what I figured, and I don't think JJ is going to want someone else driving his car everywhere."

"Hell no. His prized possession is his car. He doesn't let anyone, and I mean anyone, drive that thing."

"Do you know anything about what he has to do for paternity and with the courts?" I ask Jillian once both girls have gone back to playing.

"I don't know for sure, but I'm assuming the first step is to confirm that he is, in fact, her father. Once they've determined paternity, then rights and guardianship can be set."

"What would happen if he wasn't her father?" I ask and instantly feel a stab of pain at the thought that this little girl could potentially not be JJ's, and then she'd be ripped out of our lives. I've already become so attached to her, and it's been less than twenty-four hours since any of us even knew she existed.

"I think the state would take custody of her then. If they couldn't track down her mother, then I'd guess they'd place her with a foster home, but I don't know, to be honest."

"That would suck. I'm sure JJ is still reeling from the bombshell that dropped on his doorstep last night, but I can't imagine this precious one being taken from all of us now. That, and she's the spitting image of him. There's no way she isn't his."

"I'd have to agree with you on that one. The apple does not fall far from that tree. I'm sure everything will work out," Jillian assures me, patting my arm before she stands from the couch. "Who's ready for some lunch?" she asks the girls, and they both start rambling out things over the top of each other.

"Time-out," Jillian calls out, adding in the hand movements indicating a timeout. The girls come to a screeching halt, giving her their undivided attention. "One at a time, please," she instructs them.

"Mac and cheese!" Penny calls out.

"PB&J!" Addison says.

"I have an idea," Jillian says, looking at all of us. "What if we picked up our toys quickly then put our shoes on and go out to eat? We can even bring Auntie Ry and baby Evie with us."

"Yay!" Both girls cheer as they move to pick up their toys that are spread out from wall to wall in the living room. I'm almost shocked at how quickly they can pick everything up and get it put in the bins along the wall.

"Now, let's go potty and get shoes on," Jillian instructs them as I start to pack up Evie's things and get her secured into the car seat. She nods off once back in her seat, tucked in all nice and tight. I slip her pacifier in beside her so that I can easily find it when the need arises. With all the girls ready, we head out to Jillian's SUV and get the kids loaded. With them settled in the back, we pull out of the driveway and head to Chick-fil-A for lunch.

FIVE

JUSTIN

"Hello!" I call out as I enter from the garage
and then smack my hand over my mouth, not having even
thought that Evelyn might be sleeping, and my loud-ass
mouth might have just woken her up.

"We're in here," I hear Riley call out from the kitchen.

I toss my keys and wallet in the bowl that rests on the
table just inside the doorway that my mom said I needed
when I bought and furnished this place.

"How's it going 'round here?" I ask, taking in everything. Evelyn is content in the swing contraption, moving
her side to side. Riley is standing at the island counter,
chopping some veggies.

"We're good. I figured I'd start some dinner," she says,
smiling up at me.

"Thanks," I say just as the doorbell rings. "That should
be my lawyer and the lab to do the test," I tell her as I turn
on my heel and head for the front door.

I open it just as the bell chimes for a second time. "Hello," I greet as I open the door and find my lawyer and someone from the lab company, just as I suspected.

"JJ," William greets me. I shake his hand before they walk through the door. "This here is Margaret. She'll be taking the cheek swabs from both you and the infant. A rush order has been placed, so we'll hopefully have the results in the next few days," he tells me as I lead them into the kitchen. I watch almost dumbfounded as Margaret sets down a briefcase-looking box. Opening it, she pulls out a pair of gloves and a long Q-Tip in a plastic tube. She writes on the label before stepping directly in front of me.

"Mr. Johnson, I just need to run this along the inside of your cheek a couple of times," she informs me. I sit down since I tower over the older woman. She hardly reaches my chest, so it would be a little bit of a reach for her to swab the inside of my cheek. Thankfully, it is quick and painless, and she repeats the process with Evelyn. "Do you have any questions for me?" she asks as she packs up all of her things.

"I don't think so, just the results as soon as you have them back," I state.

"Those will go directly to you and your attorney," she tells me. "Would you like them emailed?" she asks, finishing up a form.

"Sure, or can I be called with them?" I ask, not having any clue how any of this usually works.

"I can mark down both options. Sometimes an email will get them to you a little faster, as the system automatically sends the email out when the results populate. In contrast, the phone call can't happen until we have someone available to actually call you."

"Then, an email is perfectly fine," I assure Margaret.

"Very well. The lab has been fairly fast this week, so I think you should have something back by tomorrow at this time. With the rush order and fee paid, the test will be processed as a priority."

"Thank you. The quicker, the better," I reiterate.

"Will do," she states before William sees her out for me. He returns a minute later and takes a seat at the table across from me.

"Once we have the results, as long as they confirm that you are Evelyn's father, I'll file with the courts for full custody. Do you want me also to petition the courts to revoke the mother's rights?" he asks.

"Um, I don't really know."

"The courts aren't going to like the fact that she abandoned the baby on your doorstep, but it is up to you if you want to start that process."

"Let's wait," I tell him. I have no clue what Erica's intentions are, and I'd hate to start something when she needed help and didn't know what else to do.

"All right, if that's what you'd like to do, then we'll wait. Once we have the results tomorrow, I'll be in touch," William states as he stands, offering me his hand before he turns to leave.

"That wasn't so bad," Riley says as she shakes the veggies in a bag, coating them with something.

"Nope, hopefully, we'll have some answers sooner than later."

"Do you think there's a chance the test might come back negative?"

I pull my ball cap off my head and run my fingers through my hair. It's getting a tad bit long, so I make a mental note to get it cut. "I guess there's always the possibility, but I also think she looks like me. And the timelines match up to when we were together," I answer honestly.

"I will agree that she looks a lot like you, so I'd be shocked if the test came back negative."

I watch as Riley moves around my kitchen effortlessly. She looks at home in here, like she belongs here, and that thought hits me square in the chest, almost taking my breath away. "What are you making?" I ask, changing the subject.

"Just a one sheet pan dish. Some veggies, potatoes, and chicken."

"It looks good."

"One of my favorite easy meals to make," she says, spinning to place the pan in the oven. "It will be ready in about forty-five minutes."

"Perfect," I tell her as I stand and go over to the swing. I stare at the control panel for a moment until I figure out how to turn it off. Once it comes to a stop, I unclip Evie, thankful that the buckle on this thing didn't require a fucking engineering degree to work, and cradle her in my arms. Holding a baby is still foreign to me, but Derek assured me today that the more I do it, the easier it will get. "Does she need to be changed or fed soon?"

"She might need to be changed, it's been almost two hours since I last changed her, and after that, she'll probably want a bottle. Would you like me to make you one?"

"That'd be great. I'll go change her while you do that."

"Sounds like a plan," Riley says, flashing me that pretty

smile again. I cradle Evie in my arms and turn for the living room. I snag a diaper, the wipes container, and a pad thing sticking out of the diaper bag and drop it on the couch. I lay her down gently and follow every step Riley taught me to properly change a diaper. Thankfully, no surprises happen during this diaper change. I've seen friends get peed and shit on by their kids and can only hope that never happens to me.

"Who's a good girl?" I say quietly to Evie as I zip up her outfit. She looks up at me with big, curious eyes. With her dressed, I toss the changing pad thing and the package of wipes back towards the diaper bag then prop her up on my legs that are up on the coffee table. She looks around, content as can be. I slip my finger into her hand, and she grasps ahold of it with a death grip. A moment passes as I just take her in. I have no idea if what she's doing is normal for babies this age, but I have to assume it is or else I'm sure Jillian or Riley would have mentioned something.

"Who's ready for a bottle?" Riley asks in a sing-song voice as she enters the living room. Evie turns her head to the sound of her voice. I know she's excited, as her little legs start kicking as her tongue starts peeking out of her lips like she's about to start chomping away.

"Thanks," I say as I take the bottle and then offer it to Evie. She accepts the nipple and immediately starts to suck it down greedily.

"Careful, if she does that too fast, she'll get a bellyache from the air bubbles," Riley warns. I take the bottle from her to help slow her down, and that only pisses her off and causes her to start crying. I shift her from lying on my legs to being propped in one arm like I've watched Riley hold her as she's fed her a bottle. Once she's settled in my arms, I slip the bottle back into her mouth, and she quickly quiets down as she goes back to eating.

"There's so much to learn about taking care of such a small thing," I lament as she finishes the bottle. I shift her up onto my shoulder and pat her back until she burps.

"There sure is, but you'll figure it all out. In a week you'll be a pro at all of this, I'm sure of it."

"That might be generous," I tell her.

"Just because you didn't know you have a daughter a day ago doesn't mean that you won't be a good dad, Justin," Riley tells me, and it doesn't go unmissed that she used my full first name. Hardly anyone calls me Justin. Maybe my grandmother and my mom when I'm in trouble, but other than those two, everyone calls me JJ. I usually hate it when people call me Justin, but coming from Riley, I find myself not minding one bit.

"We should discuss the nanny position," I state.

"Sure, like I said last night, I haven't been hired yet for any of the jobs I applied for, so I'm available and willing to help you out with Evie."

"I have no idea what nannies get paid, so you tell me what you charge, and we can set it up. I can contact my agent and see if they have any recommendations on accountants or services I can use to pay you correctly."

"Some of that depends on hours, if you want me to be a live-in or just here when you need me. I know you don't have a normal work schedule and that you'd need me to stay overnight at least when you're on the road, but what about when you are home?"

I digest everything she's just asked, and I have no fucking clue what to do. "I don't know the answer to that. Do you have a preference? Even when I'm in town, we've got evening games and morning practices. My schedule is all over the place."

"Okay, how about we do a trial month of me staying here. I'll be on call whenever you need me. I can plan anything I need to do around your schedule. Maybe we can sit down with a calendar and at least mark down the practices, games, and road trips that you have during that month. Then we can work my days off around those. Live-in nannies usually are provided room and board on top of their pay. I also don't mind making dinner most nights for the two of us and keeping up with some light house cleaning and laundry."

"That all sounds reasonable, does three-thousand a month sound fair?" I ask, tossing out a number.

"To start, I think so. We can reassess after the first month," she agrees readily to my offer.

"All right, it is settled then. I'll see if I can get a credit card in your name, that way, you can buy things that Evie needs, or we need here at the house. I can also pay for your gas if you have to take her places."

"That would be great. I'll head over to my place after dinner and bring some of my things over."

"Will you need help?" I offer.

"I should be fine, I don't have all that much; one car full of things, as that's all that I brought with me when I moved here a few weeks ago. I've just been using the furniture that Derek bought to furnish the condo with."

"Ah, that makes sense. If you do, just let me know, and I'm sure that we can drop Evie off with your brother for an hour."

"I've got it under control," she assures me.

I move Evie from my shoulder, where she passed out after burping. I get up and place her in the pack-n-play that Riley set up in the living room. Thankfully, she stays asleep once laid down. "Okay," I tell Riley as I grab the bottle and take it into the kitchen. I rinse it out and place it in the dishwasher. If it weren't for Jillian this morning showing me how to put one of these together, I'd probably still be standing here looking at it as a foreign object. Who knew a baby bottle could have so many confusing parts?

"Dinner should be ready in about ten minutes," Riley tells me as she starts to pull out plates and silverware.

"It smells amazing," I tell her as I suck in a deep breath, the meal filling my house with its pleasant aroma.

"Just wait until you taste it."

"If it tastes half as good as it smells, then I'm sure it will be incredible."

"Do you have any allergies I should be aware of?" she asks, setting the table.

"Nope, but I am a tad bit picky. I won't touch peas, so please don't try and make me any."

She breaks out into a giggle, and it makes my dick swell in my boxers. My eyes are drawn to the way her chest bounces up and down with each release of sound. Her tits are the perfect round size. They'd fit into my palms perfectly as my thumbs rub her nipples into tight peaks. Just large enough that I could slide my cock between them, but not too big that I'd get lost. *Fuuuuuuk*, I can't be thinking about Riley like this. I shift as discreetly as possible and adjust my cock as it threatens to bust out of my shorts. "I'll be right back," I finally grit out as I exit the kitchen as quickly as possible and head for my room. I close the door behind me and lean my back against it. My head falls back and thunks against the closed door. I suck in a deep breath through my nose and will my body to calm the fuck down. I can't be having these thoughts. Not only is Riley here to help me with my daughter, but Derek would kill me if I ever touched her. He'd probably kill me if he knew the thoughts running through my head.

Once my blood flow has finally returned to all appropriate appendages, I head back to the kitchen, where I find Riley plating up the meal she made for us. I take a seat across from her and dish up my serving. I close my eyes and take a deep breath once again, as I can feel the blood flow attempting to return to my dick. "Mmmm," she moans as her fork slips from her lips. I've never been so goddamn jealous of a fucking fork, but I am at this moment. "So, freaking good," she exclaims once she's swallowed the bite of food.

"That good, huh?" I ask, hoping that the gruffness of my voice isn't as evident to her as it is to my ears.

"Seriously, the best!" she exclaims as she readies another bite. I pick up my fork and knife and cut a bite to try for myself. As soon as the food hits my tongue, I'm done for. She wasn't joking when she said it was terrific.

"Damn, this is incredible. What else can you cook that is this amazing?" I ask, only half-joking. If she's this good of a cook, I'm going to be in trouble.

"I love to cook and experiment, and I can follow a recipe like it's my job."

We finish up our meal, mostly in silence. I try not to stare at Riley like a creeper. "I'll clean up since you cooked," I state as Riley gets up and takes her dirty dishes to the sink.

"You're sure?" she questions. "I don't mind loading my things into the dishwasher."

"I've got it, I insist."

"Okay, thanks," she says, setting the dishes down. "If you think you'll be good alone with Evie for the next hour or so, I think I'll run out to my place and pack a bag."

"We should be fine around here," I assure her.

"Sounds good. Text, or call me if anything changes. It shouldn't be too long. I can always go back another time and grab more things."

SIX

RILEY

I QUICKLY GRAB MY WALLET, KEYS, AND PHONE FROM the diaper bag and head for my car. The last twenty or so hours are catching up to me. I can't believe all that has transpired since Derek called me last night, and if someone had told me yesterday morning that I'd have a full-time nanny job as of today, I'd never have believed them.

I drive to the condo I've been living in since moving here a few weeks ago. I was so thankful when my brother and sister-in-law let me move here to be closer to them. I'm even more grateful they had this condo and have been allowing me to stay here until I could get back on my feet.

As soon as I walk in, I head for the bedroom and pull out my suitcase that hasn't been empty for all that long. Between moving here and then turning around and going out to Arizona with Jillian and the girls for part of the pre-season, I haven't had much time to get settled. I waited until a few days before we returned to start sending out applications to places, hoping to have some interviews lined up. Now that won't be necessary, or I can only hope it works out for me to be Evie's full-time nanny. I've only been around here for less than a day, and I'm already in love with her. She's such a great baby, which will make my life easy most days. Who wouldn't want to get paid to hang out with one of the cutest babies?

Once my suitcase is filled with all my clothes, I head for the bathroom and pack all the essentials from there. Since I'll probably still stay at Justin's house on my nights off, it makes the most sense to take as much of my stuff as I can. I can always pack an overnight bag to bring with me if I come back here for a random night. The more I think of it, he might want me gone on nights that I'm off. I know he's got the reputation of being a player, and I don't want to have to hear those interactions, nor do I want to encounter his conquests. Talk about an awkward situation. I shudder at the thought.

With my clothes and bathroom things all packed, I look around the bedroom then the living room to verify I don't forget anything important. I pack up my laptop and iPad, making sure I've got all the appropriate charging cords for all my devices. With everything ready to go, I load up my hands and can make it out in one trip. I place my bags into the trunk of my car and head back to JJ's.

Just as I pull out onto the main road, my phone starts ringing so I hit the accept button, allowing the call to come over the car's Bluetooth.

"Hey, honey, how's it going?" My mom's voice fills the car. "Are you getting settled in okay?"

"Hi, Mom. Everything is going great. I got a full-time nanny job effective immediately."

"Oh, that's wonderful, Ry. How old of a child or children?"

"One little girl. She's three months old and the cutest little thing ever," I gush to my mom.

"You'll have to send me a picture!" Mom says, and I can hear the excitement in her voice. "How'd you find the family?"

"That's an interesting story," I start to tell her, and go on to fill her in on the last day.

"Wow. That's crazy. Is JJ holding up with all of it?"

"He seems to be doing okay. I think that he's still in shock about it."

"I can only imagine," Mom muses. "So, you said that you're going to be living there full-time?"

"Yep, or at least for now. We're going to do a one-month trial run and see how things go. With his crazy schedule, he'll need someone that can be around all the time during the season. We're going to sit down tonight, hopefully, and if not, then tomorrow and write out a calendar with all of his games and road trips and then figure out my time off around that. But with needing to be on call, especially when he's out of town so often, I think it will be easiest to be living there."

"And Derek is okay with that arrangement?" she questions.

"I haven't told him about it. JJ and I just came up with it tonight, but he did tell JJ that he should take me up on my offer to help out. Plus, I'm a big girl, Mom. Derek doesn't get to have a say in where I work. He can try and play the overprotective big brother card all he wants, but it won't make me change my mind about the job or helping JJ."

"I'm sure he'll be fine with it then," Mom assures me.

I pull into the parking lot of Starbucks, stopping in the drive-through. "Hold on, Mom, I need to order," I tell her once it's my turn. I order quickly and then return to our conversation.

"I can let you go, I just wanted to check-in and see how things were going," she says while I'm waiting to approach the pick-up window.

"Okay, maybe I can FaceTime with you tomorrow so you can meet Evie. She's just the cutest!" I gush once again.

"Yes! Please do. I'd love to see her."

"Okay, talk then," I tell her before we disconnect our call.

I get my order and head back to JJ's house. I grab one of my bags and quietly enter the house. I can hear Evelyn crying and JJ's voice as he attempts to calm her down. I set my things down and go searching for them. I find him in the bathroom and can't stop from bursting out a laugh.

"What happened?" I ask between fits of laughter.

"She had a poop explosion," he says, looking more than a little overwhelmed with the situation. He's leaning over the tub, a screaming Evie in some water. He's got his shirt stripped off and on the floor next to him. It's soaking wet, so I can only assume that bathing her isn't going all that well.

"I think, at this point, the easiest way to get the both of you cleaned off is for you to just shower with her," I tell him, and if the shocked look on his face is telling me anything, it's that my suggestion is a crazy idea in his mind.

"I don't think so," he states matter-of-factly.

"No, seriously. Babies are easy to shower with. If it makes you feel any better, I can sit right outside the door and come in and rescue you if anything goes wrong. But both of you are covered in baby shit and need showers. The warm water will be calming to her, as well as being close to you. Babies feed off of your stress, so if you calm down, that will help Evie to calm down."

He gives me another suspicious look before he pulls her from the small amount of bathwater he'd run in the tub. "Can you hold her for a minute?" he asks, holding her up for me to take. I grab one of the towels hanging from the bar and wrap Evie in it once he hands her over. I lightly bounce her in my arms as I calmly talk to her, helping her calm down.

"How do we do this?" he asks, standing there a little dumbfounded.

"Leave your boxers on and get in. I'll hand her over, and you can wash her up. Once she's done, then I can grab her from you, and then you can finish your shower," I suggest.

"Okay," he says as he reaches in and turns on the shower. He checks the temperature of the water before stripping off his athletic shorts, leaving him in tight black boxer briefs. They don't leave much to the imagination, and I have to force myself to look away. What I wouldn't do to see him completely naked. The lines on either side of his waist that point down to his cock have me salivating and wishing he'd just drop the boxers. Once he steps into the shower, I rub my thighs together to try and dispel the ache that I'm feeling there. The one that I wish he could make go away. "I'm ready for her," he tells me, and I step closer, handing over a now calm Evie. He cradles her to his chest, allowing the warm water to hit her back. She relaxes into him just as I figured she'd do. Between the warmth of the water and the sound of his heart beating, she's a happy girl right about now.

I step away from the shower, keeping myself busy by pulling out clean towels since the two that were out, now have shit all over them. I hang a clean one for JJ on the towel bar and hold on to the one for Evie. It only takes another couple of minutes and he's got her all washed off and ready for me. I quickly wrap her up in the fluffy towel and take her into what will become the nursery, once JJ gets some permanent furniture for her in here. I get a fresh diaper on her and then pull out a clean sleeper to keep her cozy for the night. "You sure did give your daddy a run for his money tonight, Evie girl. Way to break him in," I tell her as I zip up the sleeper. I snuggle her into my arms and head for the kitchen to make her a bottle. With that established, we hunker down on the couch. I flip the TV on, finding a rerun of *Friends* to watch while she works on her bottle.

"That was the grossest thing I've ever encountered, and I'm in a locker room with twenty-four other guys daily," JJ tells me as he plops down on the couch next to Evie and me.

I laugh after seeing the disgusted look on his face. "Just wait, I'm sure something will outdo this event. But be proud, it's a rite of passage for parents to get peed, pooped, or puked on."

"I would have been just fine without ever experiencing that," he deadpans.

"At least you survived," I tell him, holding back my laughter.

"Hardly. If you wouldn't have come back when you did, we'd probably still be in that bathroom, but both of us would be crying by now," he says, reaching out and sliding the pad of his finger down Evie's cheek. She's lazily suckling on the bottle now, obviously not as hungry anymore as she starts to drift off to sleep. I take the bottle from her, shifting her to lie against my chest so I can burp her and allow her to fall into a deeper sleep. I snuggle her close, dropping some small kisses to the top of her little head. I breathe in her clean baby smell and just let it fill my senses. Not much smells better than a clean baby.

"I'll be right back, I'm going to go lay her down," I tell JJ as I stand and take Evie into my room and place her in the pack-n-play that I put in here for the time being.

"Do we need to worry about her poop-explosion?" JJ asks as I sit back down on the couch next to him.

"I don't think so; she doesn't show any other symptoms of being sick that I've noticed. Sometimes babies just have a blowout. She might even be trying to cut her first tooth, and that can cause babies to have explosions," I tell him, and his eyes go wide once again.

"I've got so much to learn."

"Don't worry, you'll learn as you go."

"What if I don't? What if I screw things up so bad for her?" he asks, and I can see the worry in his eyes.

"I'm sure every parent feels the same way. You'll get

through this. I'm sure if you called up your parents, they'd tell you they were scared shitless when they first had you. No babies come with a manual, we just have to figure things out as we go and do the best we can to shape them into productive members of society."

He runs his hands through his still damp hair as he leans forward, placing his elbows on his knees as his face falls into the palms of his hands. "I've only had her in my life for twenty-four hours, and I already feel like a failure," he finally says.

"Justin," I say his name, closing the space between us as I place my palm against his back between his shoulder blades. "You're not a failure. You've given Evie everything she needs in the last day. A safe place to be, food, and most of all, love. Not only from you, but from everyone around you that's come into contact with her so far. That little girl is lucky to have you, and you're lucky to have her. She might completely turn your world as you know it upside down, but give it a few weeks or months, and you won't remember a time without her in your life and wonder how you made it this far in life without her."

He turns his head, still resting in the palms of his hands, and looks at me. I can tell by the look in his eyes that he wants to believe me, that he wants that picture I just painted for him. All he has to do is reach out and take it and make this the best thing that's ever happened to him.

"I hope you're right," he says as he leans until his back is against the couch. He grabs my hand with his own, dwarfing my hand in the process. "I can't thank you enough for stepping in so quickly last night to help me out. I don't know what I'd be doing if it wasn't for you, Derek, and Jillian right about now."

"We're here for you; learn to accept the help when you need it. I'm not going to lie to you and tell you it will all be easy. I'm sure you can just ask Derek how hard it is to be a parent, but the good usually outweighs the bad moments, so I've been told."

"Thanks, Riley," he says, squeezing my hand in his before letting go.

"Anytime," I say in a whisper. Being this close to him, touching him like this as he looks at me with such puppy-dog eyes, has my insides shaking. My stomach feels like it's filled with butterflies as he stares at me. I watch him intently and his eyes drop ever so slowly to my lips, lingering there for a second. The tip of my tongue sneaks out and wets my lips. I can see his Adam's apple bob as he swallows hard. His eyes flick back up to mine, and the usually bright blue has darkened. I drop my eyes to his lap and can see the bulge in his sleep pants. Now I'm the one audibly gulping as I swallow. I jump up from the couch, grabbing for my phone before it clatters to the floor. "I'm going to go to bed. Get some sleep before Evie wakes up to eat again," I quickly tell him as I rush for my room.

Once inside, I close the door and lean against it, sliding down until my butt hits the floor. I don't know what's come over me today, but I can't stop thinking about Justin kissing me. What it'd be like for him to fuck me, not that I have any experience with that, seeing as I'm still a virgin. What a fucking cliché I am, the virgin nanny falling for the single dad. Not to add in the fact that he's my brother's best friend.

Derek would flip his shit if JJ and I ever did anything, but what my brother doesn't know won't kill him, either.

I finally pull myself up off the floor and head into the bathroom to get ready for bed. I slip into some sleep shorts and a tank top once my teeth are brushed and my face has been washed. I pull my long locks into a messy bun before flipping the light in the bathroom off. I use the light from my phone's screen to light the way through the room, trying to keep as quiet as I can so as not to wake up a sleeping Evie. I check on her, finding her sleeping soundly right where I laid her down earlier. I slip between the sheets and pull out my Kindle, getting lost in the pages of Kaylee Ryan's newest release.

SEVEN
JUSTIN

I wake up the next morning, my balls still blue from last night, and that's even after I rubbed one out before falling asleep. The way Riley looked at me after she caught me watching her lips had my dick so fucking hard. I could have taken her on the couch so fast, but she jumped and ran. I chastised myself the entire time I thought of her while I was stroking my cock in the shower. I can't think of her like that. She's not here for me to lust over. She's not here for me to touch. She's definitely not here for me to fuck. She's one thousand percent off-limits. She's here to take care of Evie, and I need to remember that. The last thing I need to happen is for Derek to get wind that I've been lusting over his sister and kick my ass, and for me to lose my best friend in the process. He's already warned me to stay away from her. He's privy to my playing ways. Women have always been a dime a dozen, lined up and ready to suck my cock when I need it. I don't do the settle down, flowers, and relationship game.

I have a feeling that with a baby in tow, my life is about to change.

I look down and find my cock standing at attention, tenting the sheet that covers my lower half. I guess thinking of Riley is all that it is going to take to get me hard. *Fucking great.*

I ignore my cock, slipping out of bed and heading for the bathroom. I pull on a clean pair of briefs and then some athletic shorts over them before I quietly head for the kitchen. I need some coffee this morning. As soon as I round the corner, I stop dead in my tracks. Riley is standing at the sink with Evie's head peeking over her shoulder. She's got her back to me, and I don't think she has heard me enter. She is standing there in a tank top and the smallest fucking pair of shorts known to man. They show off her ass in the most perfect way possible, and my fucking hard-on is back. *Fuck me.*

I shake my head, trying to get the visions of peeling that tank top up and off of Riley, dropping those tiny shorts to the floor and sliding inside her out of my mind. I clear my throat and move forward toward the coffee pot. "Morning," I quietly say as not to startle either of them.

"Oh, good morning, I didn't hear you get up," Riley says as she turns to face me. I do my best to not stare at her tits, but god damn, they're on full display in that tank top. I can see the slight color change where her nipple is pressing against the fabric. Evie is blocking the other one, so I only get a good look at the one, but damn do I want to see them out of that fabric. I quickly turn, pressing my hips and groin against the countertop to try and will my dick to get with the program that this isn't the time to be popping out to say hello. I snag a cup and fill it to the top, leaving only a small amount of space for a splash of creamer.

With my coffee ready, I bring it to my lips and take a tentative sip, so I don't burn the fuck out of my mouth.

"How was Evie last night?" I finally think to ask.

"She did great. Only woke up once to eat around three this morning and went right back to sleep after a diaper change and a bottle. We've been up since around seven fifteen so far this morning."

"That's good. You sleep, okay?"

"Yep, you?" she asks as she walks over to place Evie in the swing.

"Yeah," I say, sighing. "I had a little trouble falling asleep, but once I did, I slept fine."

"I hate it when that happens. I just read until I couldn't keep my eyes open anymore," she says, taking a seat across from me. "What time do you have to leave this morning?"

"Not until ten," I tell her, looking over to the clock and seeing that it's just after eight.

"Perfect. While she's content, I'm going to take a quick shower, if you don't mind. I can take her in the bathroom with me if you need me to."

"I'm good. Go take your time," I tell her, and watch as she pushes back and bounces off and down the hall. I wish I was a better man and could keep myself from watching her as she goes, but I'm not that strong, so I watch as her ass bounces down the hall and disappears into her room. *I am so fucked.*

I finish my cup of coffee, then get up to refill it and

make myself some breakfast. I pull out everything to whip up a veggie and meat-filled omelet. I look over at Evie, swinging away across from me, and can't help but smile at her. She's so content, looking around as the swing moves her back and forth. Once my food is done, I set it on the table and then pull the swing over next to me.

"Who's a pretty girl?" I ask my daughter as she starts to blow spit bubbles at me. I reach out and run my finger down her face, and she reaches up and grabs hold of it, pulling it into her mouth to suck and chew on. Maybe Riley was right in that she's already teething. I can remember when Derek's girls were babies, and they'd always be trying to chew on everything when they were cutting teeth.

I let her chew on my finger for another few minutes while I do my best to eat one-handed. This isn't as easy as some people make it look, and my respect for all the parents out there just increased tenfold.

I finish up my breakfast, pulling my hand back from Evie so I can clean up my dishes. She doesn't like that too much, and by the time I've got everything put away, she's got a good cry going. I rescue her from the swing, and she immediately calms down once in my arms. "Is that all you needed, baby girl?" I ask her. She lays her head against my chest and snuggles in as I take her into the living room. I pull out the floor contraption thing that Jillian said was for tummy time and place her down on it as I lay on the floor next to her. She looks around, taking in her surroundings before letting out one hell of a wail of a cry. "Do you not like that?" I ask, swooping her back into my arms as I sit upon the floor. She once again settles down, so I back up until I've got my back against the couch and place her on my legs. I let her grab my finger once again, and she pulls it to her mouth, chewing on it with her gums.

"How's it going?" Riley's voice fills the silence awhile later. I look up and find her standing a few feet away, just watching the two of us. She's dressed in some shorts and a flowy tank top, nothing special, but damn does she look like a million bucks. She's got her hair down; she dried it, as it's cascading around her shoulders in perfect waves. I take her in from her bare toes and the cutest fucking feet I've ever seen on a woman. *When have I started thinking feet were cute? My damn mind is going crazy.* My gaze moves up her long legs, just beginning to show a slight tan to them, seeing that we're just coming into spring and the hot summer weather hasn't quite shown up yet. My eyes roll over her hips, thin waist, over her curves, finally landing on the smile that's filling her face.

"We're good," I finally croak out, realizing I hadn't answered her question. "Just spending some time together that doesn't include being shit on."

"Give it a little bit of time, and that will be a long distant memory."

"One I hope never repeats itself," I say as I tickle Evie's belly, getting a broad smile from her. I do it again and light up when she lets out a little laugh along with her smile. My heart cracks open at the sound, and I think I can get used to this whole dad schtick.

I look up and see Riley has her phone out and pointed in our direction. She turns it around and shows me the picture that she snapped of Evie and me together.

Looking at the image, you'd never guess that this was a new thing for me. I look like such a natural in the picture, and that scares the shit out of me. "Can you text that to me?"

"Of course," she says just as I hear my cell ding with the incoming text. "Hey, do you care if I send pictures of Evie to my mom? She wanted to see her, but I wanted to check with you first before I did so."

"Of course," I tell her and let her question sink in. I've got a daughter to protect, and that means from the ugly that can be social media. "Thanks for asking first. I didn't even think about sharing pictures of her, so maybe we'll keep her off social media for now. Especially until we have the official test results and court orders."

"Absolutely, and I'm sure that once word gets out that you've got a kid, the media is going to be all over it. It will probably be hard to keep it all a secret once your attorney files anything with the courts. I'm sure your name coming up in court documents will flag some reporters' search on you."

"Yeah," I tell her, thinking about the media shit storm that will cause. "I might need to reach out to my PR rep to get ahead of everything, ask the media to give me privacy right now."

"That probably wouldn't be a bad thing. Do you think that Erica would possibly go to the media? Try and sell her story?"

"It's possible, money will make most people talk."

"Justin, I just want you to know that I'd never talk to anyone or sell you out. I just wanted to be upfront with that right now. I know what it's like to have a family member in the media spotlight."

"Thanks for that. The thought never crossed my mind that you would, but thanks for that reassurance." I look back down at Evie as I take a few deep breaths. I need to get out in front of all of this. "Do you mind taking over here so I can go call my PR rep and lawyer to see what we can do to keep things out of the media and hopefully keep Erica from going to the media?"

"Of course," she says, leaning down and picking Evie up. "Hey, baby girl, did you miss me?" she asks Evie as she kisses the top of her head.

I stand and grab my cell from the end table. I scroll through my contacts until I find my PR company's contact. I press the call button and wait as the line rings. It only takes a few rings, and a voice comes over the line.

"Good morning, Executive PR this is Tracey, how can I help you today?"

"Good morning, Tracey, this is Justin Johnson. I've got a personal matter that I wanted to discuss with someone that we might need to get ahead of with the media, is anyone available?"

"Of course, let me get you in touch with Logan," she says and then places me on hold or transfers the call.

"Mr. Johnson, how can I help today?" Logan asks in the way of a greeting.

I give him the rundown of what's transpired over the last twenty-four hours and my concerns to keep things quiet if the media was to get knowledge of things going forward, plus how we'd handle it if Erica were to sell a story to the press.

"I'll be in touch with your attorney and manager and draw up a plan. Depending on how things play out, it might be in your best interest if we release a press statement ahead of any court documents becoming public. Something simple that states you've recently become a father and are enjoying getting to know your daughter. We'll ask for privacy during this time. Most of the time, the media is willing to accept blanket statements and give you the space you've asked for," Logan tells me.

"I'm fine with all of that, and at a later date, I might even be willing to sit down for an interview, but that will need to be down the road. I need time to adjust to being a single father."

"I completely understand, and when the time comes that you're ready for something like that, I can handle setting that up with a trusted reporter who we know will allow us to vet all questions and control what is and isn't shown, whether it be a print piece or one that is aired on TV. I'll be in touch with the plan, possibly by the end of today."

"Thanks, Logan," I tell him before we hang up.

Knowing a plan is in the works to keep Evelyn safe, I head for my bedroom and get dressed for practice. Even with all that is going on, I can't skip out on my responsibilities. I've got training today and a game tomorrow afternoon, and three days after that, we leave for a road trip.

"All good here?" I ask Riley as I slip my shoes on.

"We're all good," she says, smiling up at me from the

floor where Evie's lying on her belly on the tummy time mat. She isn't screaming like she was when I tried it, but I realize now that I'd placed her on her back, and Riley has her on her stomach. "Have a good practice."

"Thanks. Have fun, and I'll see you girls, later," I call out as I pick my bag up and head out the door.

"How'd the night go?" Derek asks, taking a seat next to me on the bench in front of our lockers.

"Good. Riley said Evie only got up once to eat."

"She going to watch her full-time for you?" he asks.

"Yeah, we discussed everything last night. I've got to find out if there's an agency or something that I can pay her through that will handle all the taxes and shit that I've got no clue how to handle. We're going to test it for a month and go from there. With it being the beginning of the season, it isn't like I can just hire someone to work Monday through Friday, eight to five. I need someone that can be around when we're out of town and late when we have evening games. You know how it is. This isn't a normal schedule type of job."

"It sure isn't," he muses. "I'm sure she'll do a good job taking care of Evie for you. Just stay away from her," he says, giving me the evil older brother stare.

"She's Evie's nanny. I don't plan on fucking that arrangement up," I tell my best friend, hoping that the words will sink into my own brain. If I keep telling myself that she's off-limits, then maybe I'll stop lusting after her.

"Ready to hit the field?" he asks, standing and grabbing his glove from the top shelf of his locker.

"I was born ready," I cockily reply, standing and grabbing my glove and following him out of the locker room and into the dugout. I pull on my catchers' equipment, and we get to work warming up.

Ninety minutes later, I'm drenched in sweat and am ready to hit the weight room for an hour of lifting. "How's the arm feeling?" I ask Derek as we enter the dugout.

"Great. Like I'll be on fire for my next start." He smirks —*such a cocky bastard.*

"You'd better be," I tell him as we enter the weight room along with a few of the other guys on the team. The room is filled with grunts mixed with the music pumping through the speakers.

I make it through the workout and am more than ready to hit the showers after today's practice and workout session. We've got a team meeting before I can leave for the day, and I'm hoping that by the time that happens, I'll have results from the lab.

"You want to bring Evie over for dinner tonight?" Derek asks as we push out the doors and into the players' parking lot an hour later.

"Sure, let me just make sure Riley hasn't already made something," I tell him, pulling my phone out of my pocket.

"She's cooking for you?" he asks, an edge to his voice.

"I didn't ask her to, she offered. No need to go all papa bear on my ass again," I say, chuckling at his instant alerted awareness when it comes to anything I say about his sister. I'm almost surprised he brought her over and suggested she be Evie's nanny if he's so worried about the two of us being alone together so much.

"Don't get used to it. Riley can't live with you forever, and she isn't your fucking maid."

"I'm well aware of that," I deadpan. "But I'm also not going to look a gift horse in the mouth and turn down a home-cooked meal when she does cook."

"All right, I'll let Jillian know that the three of you might be joining us for dinner," he calls out as he slides into the driver's seat of his truck. I'm parked right next to him, and I sink into the driver's seat of my sports car. Riley texts me back, letting me know she hadn't started anything and that she can just put the chicken she has defrosting in the fridge and make it tomorrow. I roll down my window to call out to Derek.

"We'll be there. What time do you want us to come by?" I ask.

"Five, maybe five thirty," he says.

"Sounds good, see you then. Want me to bring anything?"

"Just my niece and sister." He smirks. His words hit me straight in the chest. How easy he's accepted Evie into my life and considers her his niece.

I head home, still not having heard anything from my attorney or the lab on the results of the test. I pull into the driveway about ten minutes later and find myself excited to get inside and see how the day went for Evie and Riley. I grab my bag from the passenger seat and head into the house. It's quiet, so I do my best to keep it that way. I find Riley in the living room watching TV and folding a basket of laundry. Looking around, I don't see Evie anywhere, so she must be sleeping in the bedroom.

"Hey," I greet, pulling Riley's attention to me.

"How was practice?" she asks.

"Pretty normal. Did my best to kick your brother's ass out on the field." I snicker.

"He can use an ass-kicking every once in a while," she muses.

"Nah, he's one of the best pitchers I've ever played with, and I'm not just saying that because he's your brother and my best friend."

"I know, just don't tell him that too often, or it will just make his ego grow. He's already cocky enough as it is."

"I won't argue with you there," I say, laughing. "Evie sleeping?" I ask.

"Yep, went down for an afternoon nap about thirty minutes ago. We had a fun day. Had some tummy time, some swing time, went for a walk outside, followed by a short nap in the late morning and now this afternoon one. The crib, changing table and car seat bases were all delivered today as well. The delivery guys got everything set up for us, so she's napping for the first time in her crib. Exciting times 'round here," she says as she pushes the basket of folded clothes away from her as she stands and picks it up, presumably to put it away.

"Sounds like a fun day. Did everything fit in the room okay?"

"It did, you'll have to go take a look at it once she's awake." She says as she walks down the hall, setting the basket down outside of Evie's room. "As she gets older, she'll start staying awake for longer periods, as well as getting more and more interested in playing with toys."

"Anything else I need to buy now for her?" I ask, knowing that Jillian picked up things she said would be essential to get us by for now.

"I actually started a list on Amazon of things that I've thought of that would be nice to get. I just add them to the list when I think of them so that I can show you, and we can order them when needed."

"That works, and I don't mind you picking up anything that will make our lives easier. The cost isn't an issue," I remind her. I make upwards of fifteen million a year, so a handful of baby items will hardly put a dent into my bank account.

"Any news on the test results?" she asks.

"Nothing yet. I was hoping that we'd have something by now."

"I'm sure it will come through soon," she assures me.

"I hope so," I tell her as she walks away down the hall. I head into the kitchen, grab a bottle of water and an apple from the bowl on the counter.

"Did you get groceries?" I ask, not remembering apples being here earlier.

"Just a few things. When Evie and I were out on our walk, we stopped at the little farmers market in the parking lot of the school and picked up a few items."

"Oh, nice. I didn't even know they had that."

"The one vendor said that this was their first week back for the season. She said that as the summer goes on, they'll get more vendors that come out and lots more things to choose from."

"Makes sense," I tell her before biting into the apple. "Pretty good," I say after swallowing my first bite.

"They are, I can try and get some more next week if they have any left."

"I'll try and remember to get to the bank and get some cash out to leave for you to have for things like that."

"I don't mind buying a few things. I'd have to spend money on food if I wasn't living here."

"I know, but I also don't expect you to spend your money on food for Evie or me, so if it's something that either of us would end up having, let me pay for it."

"Okay," she concedes easily. "What time did you want to head over to my brother's?"

"He said to come over between five and five thirty."

"Sounds good. Evie should be up before then," she says, making herself busy by starting to unload the dishwasher. I step in and help, not wanting her to feel like she has to do everything around here.

"Thanks," she says once we've got it emptied.

"Anytime," I tell her. There's only a foot or so between the two of us, and it's as if we both notice that fact at the same time. Once we do, it's almost as if all the air in the room is sucked out. The crackling sexual tension between the two of us could be cut with a knife; it is so thick. I can feel the sparks buzzing and know deep down that it's only a matter of time before they ignite if I don't put space between the two of us.

The silence is shattered when my phone starts ringing

from my pocket. I pull it out and see my attorney's name flashing on the screen, so I immediately accept the call and press the phone to my ear.

"Hello."

"Justin, William here. I've got the results of the test in front of me. The lab has confirmed that you are, in fact, Evelyn's father, so congratulations!" he says joyfully into the phone. The emotions of the last two days hit me square in the chest. Everything confirmed, and this little girl who was dropped on my doorstep and has quickly wormed her way right into my heart is mine to keep forever. "As we discussed before, I'll move forward with filing for full custody on your behalf. I had a conversation with Logan and think that it's a good idea if we have him release the statement to get out in front of this."

"I'll do whatever you guys think is best. I just want to keep Evie safe. When do you plan to file the paperwork?" I ask, taking a seat on one of the barstools tucked under the counter.

"I'll file first thing Monday morning when the courts open."

"Okay," I say, blowing out a huge breath. Having the results of the test has lifted an enormous weight from my chest that I didn't even realize had been there.

"Do you have any further questions for me?" he asks.

"Any luck with tracking Erica down?"

"Not that I'm aware of. If we don't make contact by Tuesday, I planned to get our PI on the case to track her down. The courts will also want her found to serve her with the custody paperwork."

"Sounds good. Let me know if you need anything else from me," I tell him.

"Will do, and if you hear from Erica in the meantime, please let me know."

"I can do that."

"I'll be in touch on Monday once everything is filed," William tells me.

Holy shit. I'm a dad.

"So..." Riley prompts, a massive smile on her face. I didn't even realize she'd left the room, but she now has an alert Evie in her arms.

"It's confirmed, she's mine forever," I tell her.

"Yay! Did you hear that, Evie girl? You've got yourself a daddy forever, baby girl," Riley says as she dances around my kitchen with my daughter in her arms. I can't keep the emotions inside any longer and find myself laughing at their antics as tears stream down my face.

"How about some snuggles and love from your daughter?" Riley says, coming to stand next to me. She hands Evie over to me, and I pull my daughter in, holding her tight to my chest as I let the tears fall. I'm not even worried right now that I'm a fucking emotional mess in front of Riley. I know she's not going to be out telling anyone about this moment. I look up and see her wiping at her own eyes as she watches the two of us. "Congratulations, Justin. She's lucky to have you."

"I'm pretty sure I'm the lucky one," I tell her honestly.

"So, does this mean that you'll be stopping the man-whore ways of the past?" she asks. Her question isn't said in a mean way, but I can hear the curiosity lacing her question.

"I guess it does. I've got to set a good example for my daughter," I tell her honestly. What I don't tell her is that the only woman I've even thought about warming my bed lately is her. I haven't even thought about another woman in the past couple of days.

"I'm sure you'll do a great job at that," she says, and I know she's being honest.

"Thanks," I tell her as my phone starts to ring again. I look down and see that it's my mom calling, and I realize at that moment that I haven't talked to my parents in a week. They have no clue the events of the past two days, so I'm about to blow their freaking world.

"Hey, Mom," I greet as I answer the phone.

"How's my favorite son?" she asks.

"I'm your only son," I deadpan as I always do when she says that.

"Semantics," she says, humor lacing her voice.

"Hey, Mom, is Dad around? I've got something that I want to talk to both of you about."

"Yeah, he's out in the garage puttering around. I can go grab him."

"That'd be great, then let's switch over to FaceTime," I suggest.

"Is everything okay?" she asks, and I can tell she's worried now.

"Yep, it is great," I assure her.

"Paul, come in here. JJ's on the phone and wants to talk with both of us." I hear her call out to my dad. "He's coming, switch us over to FaceTime." I hand Evie over to Riley and hit the button to switch us over. I head into the living room, motioning for Riley to follow me. I keep her and Evie from the view of the camera for now. I sit down on the couch just as both of my parents come into the screen.

"So, what's up?" Dad asks me.

"Well," I say, all of a sudden, the words escaping me on how to drop this news on my parents.

"Spit it out, Justin," my mom says, picking up on my hesitation.

"Two nights ago, a chick shows up on my doorstep that I hung out with a few times last year with a baby. She said that I was the baby's father and that she couldn't handle being a single parent, and she left. Derek and Jillian, along with Derek's sister, Riley, all stepped in and have been helping me the last two days while I figure everything out. I just got the call from my attorney with the paternity test that proves that she is my daughter. He's going to file with the courts Monday for full custody."

"Holy shit," my mom says, obviously shocked at what I've just told her.

"Would you guys like to meet your granddaughter?"

"Of course!" Mom practically screeches out. Riley hands over Evie, and I do my best to prop her up in the view of the camera. "Oh, Justin!" Mom exclaims. "She's so precious. What is her name?"

"Evelyn, but we've been calling her Evie for short."

"Congratulations, son!" Dad pipes in.

"We'll have to come out so we can meet her," Mom says, excitement falling off her in waves. She's practically bouncing in her seat.

"You're welcome to come out whenever you want. I've

got a road trip coming up this week, but Evie and Riley will be here," I tell them.

"What are your plans for childcare moving forward?" Mom asks.

"I've hired Riley as a full-time live-in nanny for now. We're giving the live-in portion of it a month trial to make sure that it works for all of us, but with my hectic and sporadic schedule, I kind of need someone that can be here all the time or at least be here for my travel schedule."

"That makes sense," Dad states.

"Paul, pull out your calendar. When can we go to Indy and meet our new granddaughter?" Mom asks him, tapping him on the arm until he does as she's asked. I watch as he pulls out the pocket calendar he still insists on carrying around and using from the breast pocket of his shirt.

"Well, with Justin leaving town, do you want to wait to head out when he's back or show up when he's gone?" Dad asks her. "Our calendar is fairly empty, and the few things I've got down are things that can be moved."

"Oh, I'll look and see if we can get flights for Monday or Tuesday. That way, we arrive before you leave town, and we can stay for a week or two."

"If you want," I tell my mom, knowing that she's going to do whatever in the hell she wants. I also realize she's excited to come to meet her first grandchild.

"I'll forward you the flight info once I can get something booked."

"Okay, but only if you let me pay for the tickets," I tell her, giving her as pointed of a look as I can via the camera.

"You know you don't have to pay for everything for us," Mom chides.

"It's the least I can do," I remind her. They sacrificed things while I was growing up so that I could play ball. Always traveling all over the place for travel ball, shelling money out for gear, and hotels, countless meals at ball field concession stands, or on the road between fields and home. When I signed my first contract and received that first bonus for doing so, I paid off their mortgage the very next day. I also sent two brand new vehicles to their house, no option left off of either of them. My parents weren't poor, but they weren't rolling in cash, either. We lived comfortably, and I'll always be thankful for the life they gave me growing up. Being an only child, they devoted their lives to me and the sport I loved playing. Thankfully, that dedication paid off, and I've done my best to repay them in the last few years for all they did for me growing up.

"Okay," Mom finally concedes. "I'll put them on the card you left here."

"Thank you. I can't wait for you to meet Evie. She's a pretty chill baby, and I'm sure you'll love her."

"I already do. Send me some pictures," Mom states.

"Of course," I tell her before we end the call. I text her right away the picture that Riley snapped of Evie and me, as well as a couple of images that I have taken of her.

"You ready to pack up and head over to my brother's?" Riley asks a few minutes later. I didn't realize it was already that time.

"Yeah," I tell her, standing up and handing Evie over as Riley stands next to me with her arms out and open, asking for her. She places her in the car seat and gets her all strapped in. She slings the diaper bag over her shoulder, and before she can pick Evie up, I slip my arm through the handle of the seat and carry it out to my car. I snap her car seat into the base on the first try and feel on top of the world. This dad shit is not so bad, after all.

"Your parents were so cute," Riley says as we back out of the driveway.

"You might change your mind after they've been here for a few days," I say on a laugh.

"They can't be that bad, and you've met my parents before," she says, giving me a pointed look.

I laugh at her facial expression. "Your parents aren't that bad. But I guess we all feel that way about our parents. I just don't have any clue what to expect out of mine, if I'm honest. I don't think that they expected me ever to have kids of my own, or at least none anytime soon."

"They never gave you a hard time about settling down and having kids?"

"Not really. My mom mentioned it a few times, but I shut that shit down pretty quickly. Now, look at me." My eyes flick over to Riley and then up to the rearview mirror as I look at the car seat strapped in my back seat. I can see Evie in the reflection of a little mirror that hangs from the head-rest that she faces.

"Sometimes, things happen for a reason. We might not know what that reason is, but life has a way of working things out," Riley states.

"How do you always look at the positives?" I ask. Riley is a half-glass full type of person.

"Looking at the negatives all the time would make life suck. Take my life, for example. I grew up in the shadows of a brother that showed athletic abilities from a young age. There were rumblings of him being good enough to go pro before he even entered high school, and here I am, the girl that can't even throw a ball ten feet. I did my best to be my own person and not be in his shadow, but that isn't always easy when he's the town's golden child. Everyone knew who he was, and that was hard sometimes. Once I went off to college, it wasn't so bad since we didn't go to the same place, nor was he around all the time by then. He was already in the pros and making a name for himself. When things went south with my job, I could have let it get me down, but instead, I pulled up my bootstraps and moved on to better things. I didn't allow it to get me down too much, and I can't say that I'm unhappy with everything that's transpired since I moved here, and that's all because of a bad situation that I left."

"Wow," is all I can think to say to her little speech. "I can't say I'm sorry that you had to move here, either. I'd be lost without your help."

"If I weren't here, you'd have found someone else to help you."

"Yeah, but not someone I know I can trust as much as I can with you," I tell her honestly as I pull into Derek and Jillian's driveway.

EIGHT
RILEY

I GET OUT OF THE CAR AND GRAB EVIE'S DIAPER BAG while JJ works on unsnapping the car seat from the base. Before I make it up the stoop, the door flies open, and my niece, Penelope, is standing there in a princess dress and a huge smile on her face. "Auntie Ry!" she yells out, running and jumping into my arms.

"Hey, baby girl!" I say, swinging her into my arms. Her little legs wrap around my torso and her arms go around my neck as I stand up to my full height. "Did you miss me?" I ask against Penny's throat.

"Of course, I did, Aunt RyRy," she says, squeezing me tighter.

"Where's your sister?" I ask as I set Penny back down on the ground.

"She's playing," she states matter-of-factly.

"Should we go find her and play with her?" I suggest.

"Sure!" Penny says, tugging on my hand and pulling me into the house. I look back at JJ and see that he's finally got

72

Evie's car seat out of the base and is walking up behind us. I follow my niece into the house, calling out to Jillian as I pass by the kitchen, and into the living room where my other niece, Addison, is twirling around in circles as she dances along to the music coming from the princess show on the TV.

"Auntie Ry!" she calls out excitedly once she spots me, mid twirl. She wobbles when she comes to a screeching stop, the dizziness finally catching up to her from spinning so much.

"Addison," Jillian scolds from behind me. "I told you not to be spinning so much. You're going to make yourself sick doing that, and I don't want to be cleaning up puke."

"Sorry, Momma," she answers, jutting her bottom lip out in a pout. I hold my hands out for her to come to me, and that morphs her pout back into a smile.

"How's my big girl today?" I ask once Addison is in my arms and hugging me tightly.

"Good," she says, her voice muffled by my hair.

"How about we play a game?" I suggest to both my nieces a moment later. The scolding from Mom forgotten about after a few minutes of cuddles from their favorite aunt.

"Yay!" They both cheer as they start to bounce up and down in front of me.

"What should we play?" I ask.

"Barbies!" Addison suggests while Penny states, "Babies!" at the same time.

I look back and forth between the two of them, trying to determine how best to diffuse the situation since they want separate things. "How about this..." I tell them, tapping my index finger against my lips as I stall, thinking my plan over again. "How about we play babies until it's time to wash up for dinner, and then after dinner, we can play with Barbies until it's time to clean up for bed."

They both seem to think my suggestion is an excellent idea as they both turn and start picking up the toys that are scattered around the living room before pulling out the baby doll things. Before I know it, I've got many baby dolls in all states of dress piled on my lap. One is supposedly sleeping, another one being fed a bottle, and yet another in need of a diaper change.

"Looks busy in here," JJ's deep voice breaks into the chatter from the girls.

"Just get used to it," I say as I look up at him. He's got Evie in his arms facing out as she takes in her surroundings. She's got her fist in her mouth as she sucks and chews on it, drool starting to run down her arms and chin. She's teething if those sighs indicate anything. "Before you know it, she'll be playing with baby dolls; dressing, and undressing them. Wanting to do their hair and makeup," I tell him and practically watch as the color drains from his face.

"Maybe she'll be a tomboy and want to play with baseballs and trucks," he tosses out.

"Maybe, but don't be surprised if your house is puking pink and sparkles within the year," I tease him slightly. "You're going to have to get used to sharing your bachelor pad with a girl now."

The sound that rumbles from his chest startles Evie, and she gives a little yell of her own. "It's okay, Evie," I call out to her, "Daddy didn't mean to upset you." Her eyes find mine from the few feet that separate us, and she gives me a gummy smile as her arms and legs start to kick.

"Want me to take her?" I offer, and hold my arms out for her.

"Sure," he agrees and takes a few steps closer before handing her over. I move some of the baby dolls from my lap, making room for Evie. I prop her up between my legs, allowing her head and neck to rest against my thigh. The girls immediately swarm around me, waiting to get in close to her. "Careful," I remind both of them as I get Evie situated.

"Derek said that dinner should be ready in about ten," JJ says once I've got Evie settled and the girls being gentle as they make silly faces at her, trying to coax a smile or laugh from her. She gives in quickly to them, her little eyes bouncing between the girls.

"Sounds good. I'm starving, so perfect timing," I tell him before turning my attention back to the three little girls all around my lap.

***

"THANK YOU FOR YOUR HELP TONIGHT," JILLIAN SAYS as we both plop down on opposite ends of the couch. The girls are both fast asleep for the night.

"Of course," I assure her. "How are you feeling?" I ask, figuring that running after two active little girls while being pregnant can't be easy, especially with how busy my nieces are.

"Tired," she says on a laugh. "This gestating another human is no joke, and I always forget just how tiring it is. I feel like I could take a nap for the next three days, and I'd still be tired."

"I can only imagine," I tell her. I don't have the expertise on what it's like to grow a tiny human inside of me; I can only imagine from when I've experienced friends or family that have been pregnant around me.

"How are things going with JJ and Miss Evie?" she asks. The guys are outside drinking a beer on the patio. Evie is sleeping in the swing in the corner of the living room. I look over at her, peaceful, as the machine sways side to side.

"Good. I'm glad that JJ got the results today. I think that knowing for sure that she's his lifted a weight from his shoulders. That, and he was so damn cute with her this afternoon."

"He's taken to her a lot faster than I expected him to," Jillian says.

"You should have seen him introducing his parents to her over FaceTime. It was the best thing ever. I almost felt bad for being there for such a personal moment."

"You have nothing to feel bad about. You've helped him out of a big bind. Without someone that can step in and basically be a surrogate mother for Evie, especially with JJ's work schedule, he'd have to take a leave of absence or retire completely, and we all know that he isn't ready to do that, he's still in the prime of his career."

"He'd also be miserable if he retired now. He'd resent having to do so, well before he needs to."

"That's for sure. Everything between the two of you

going okay?" she asks, a raised eyebrow accompanying the question.

"Yes..." I say, drawing out the word. "Why wouldn't it be?" I ask.

"Two consenting adults, a lot of time alone together..." she says, trailing off.

"God, no!" I practically shriek at my sister-in-law. "JJ would never look at me that way," I tell her, shaking my head side to side. "There's no way I'm his type, even if I wanted to be."

"Why do you think that?"

"A few reasons," I say, blowing out a huge breath. "First off, he's my brother's best friend. Isn't there some unwritten rule against that?" I ask.

"Rules are meant to be broken," Jillian states. "And think of all the books you've read that are about brother's best friends falling for the younger sister. One of the best damn tropes, in my opinion. But I digress, continue with your reasoning why the two of you can't be a thing."

"I'm his employee. Absolutely, not the usual one-night stand he's used to. Kind of hard to be that type when I'm still a virgin," I admit.

"Oh, honey. Don't sell yourself so short. None of those reasons that you just gave me should be anything to stand in your way. If something develops between the two of you, I say go for it. Will Derek be pissed? Probably, for a hot second, but I'll be here to help calm him down and remind him that you're a grown-ass woman who can make her own decisions. Even if they're not the ones that he'd make for you, and then I'd remind him that JJ is his best friend, and yes, the man was once a manwhore chasing anything in a skirt, but people can change, and I think that little girl over there has already started that change in him."

"I still don't see anything transpiring, so I'm not going to dwell on it. He's got a lot on his plate right now, and I don't think a relationship is on his radar."

"Just give it some time. He'll realize how good he's got it with you there, cooking all his meals, taking care of his daughter. Think of how easy it would be for you to just slip into taking care of him as he takes care of you," she says, wiggling her eyebrows at me.

"You suck," I say, busting out laughing as I toss a throw pillow across the couch in Jillian's direction.

"Or I just like to tell it how I see it. I've only been around the two of you together a few times, but I've already witnessed him tracking you with his eyes when he thinks no one is paying attention. Something is stirring in his mind. He's maybe not come out and admitted or tried to act on those thoughts and desires, but they're running through his mind."

"Are you sure?" I ask, not believing what she's saying. Does JJ watch me?

"Positive. That man has got it bad for you, he just doesn't know how to act on it, or is waiting until the right time to act on it."

"I don't know," I say, biting on my thumbnail.

"Oh, before I forget. Do you think you can come over on Thursday for a couple of hours and watch the girls? I have an OB appointment and don't want to drag them with me.

Derek will, of course, be out of town that day on the road trip."

"Sure," I tell her as I pull my phone from where I have it tucked between my leg and the couch. I open the calendar app and add in a note so that I don't forget. "What time is your appointment?"

"I think at ten, but I'll verify that and let you know for sure. My phone is just in the kitchen plugged in, so I can't check at the moment."

"Not a problem. I'll just put in to plan to come over by around nine, that way, you have plenty of time to get out of here and arrive on time."

"Thanks, you're a lifesaver."

"Of course," I tell her, and I mean it. I'd do anything for family.

NINE
JUSTIN

I HEAD INTO THE HOUSE TO CHECK ON THE GIRLS AND grab a glass of water. The beer went down smooth, but I don't need to be overindulging when I've got to drive home soon. I can hear Riley and Jillian talking from the living room, and stop dead in my tracks when I hear just what they're talking about.

"Rules are meant to be broken," Jillian states. "And think of all the books you've read that are about brother's best friends falling for the younger sister. One of the best damn tropes, in my opinion. But I digress, continue with your reasoning why the two of you can't be a thing."

"I'm his employee. Absolutely, not the usual one-night stand he's used to. Kind of hard to be that type when I'm still a virgin."

Virgin. Fuckkkkkk.

All I can think of now is touching her and being the only man to do so. To know that she's perfect, completely untouched by another man, has my cock swelling in my pants. I shake my head, trying to shake those thoughts from my mind, but all I can think about is her on her knees, those plump lips wrapped around my cock as it slides in, hitting the back of her throat until I'm coming down it. I can also picture pinning her up against a wall, dropping to my own knees as I devour her pussy until she's screaming my name and limp from her orgasm.

"Dude, what are you doing?" Derek's voice breaks my trance as he opens the door.

"I'm just grabbing something," I tell him, forcing myself to walk into the kitchen and stop listening in on the girls' conversation. I grab a glass and fill it with ice and water from the fridge dispenser. I down the water in one tip of the glass, refilling it before I go back outside to join him.

"What was that all about?" he asks once I sit back down next to him.

"Nothing, just thought I heard Evie," I lie to him, hoping that he doesn't call me on it.

"I'm sure the girls got everything under control."

"Yeah," I tell him as I drop my head back and close my eyes. I'm so fucked. All I want is to fuck my best friend's little sister. The one woman who's definitely off-limits to me, and it isn't like I can talk to him about it. She's *his* damn sister.

"What's got you all tied up all of a sudden?" he asks, obviously picking up on the change in my demeanor.

"Everything," I tell him, trying to be as honest as I can without blurting out that I can't get Riley out of my thoughts. "My life has literally been tossed upside down in the last few days and it's finally setting in."

"I'll give you that one, for sure," he agrees, tipping back the beer bottle in his hands as he finishes it off. "Just give it a little bit of time, and it will be your new normal."

"What if I fuck it all up?" I ask him, looking him in the eye for the first time since I came back out here.

"We all make mistakes, it's how we move forward and learn from those mistakes that allows us to grow as people," he tells me. "And just remember that kids don't come with owner's manuals. What works with one doesn't work with the next. I won't lie and tell you it's all puppies and rainbows and carefree days, but it's all worth it. I wouldn't change anything about my life, and you've seen me at my worst. I'd take all those bad days over again if it got me right back to where I am now. Knowing that I've got that woman inside there by my side makes life worth living. Knowing that I've got two of the best little girls calling me Daddy and another one on the way is the best thing in the world. Just wait until Evie is old enough to call you Dad for the first time, or tell you that she loves you. It will bring you to your fucking knees, brother."

"I just don't want to fuck it all up," I state mindlessly.

"We won't let you," he says confidently. "Those two women in there will keep you and me on the straight and narrow."

"I hope you're right," I muse as I squeeze the back of my neck, attempting to relieve the tension that has built up.

We sit in silence for a few minutes, and my mind races as everything that has happened is on a constant loop. I can't believe I'm sitting here while my *daughter* is inside sleeping in a swing.

"I should probably get going," I tell Derek as I stand back up and turn to walk back into the house so that I can get my girls home. Just as I reach the door, the thought slams into me that I just thought of Evie *and* Riley as *my girls*. The scary part of that thought was how right it felt. How right this could all be if she could be mine. If we could make something between the two of us work. But I know that will never happen, not unless I want to lose my best fucking friend in the process.

"Yeah," Derek agrees. "I'm ready to take my wife to bed."

"I'm sure you are. You know you can't knock her up again right now, right?" I give him shit.

"All I can say is pregnancy hormones, especially now that she's in the second trimester, are fucking crazy."

"I'll have to take your word for it," I tell him as I push the door open. I've never spent much time around a pregnant woman unless you count Jillian, and it isn't like I've ever tried to get her into my bed.

Derek follows me inside, both of us heading for the living room where the girls are relaxing on the couch. Thankfully, their conversation has moved on from what I overheard just a little bit ago. I couldn't imagine hearing any more, especially with Derek by my side. He'd be pissed if he knew Jillian was pushing Riley toward me.

"Hey, you ready to get out of here?" I ask once there's a break in the conversation between Riley and Jillian.

"Sure," she says, pushing the throw blanket off of her legs. She arches her back in a stretch before standing, and my mind goes right into the fucking gutter, thinking of many other ways I could get her to bend like that for me, off a bed, the wall, a kitchen counter. Any surface will do, in my opinion.

I grab Evie's car seat and ready the straps to slide her in. I can only hope that dealing with my daughter will help the blood flow redirect where it is headed, so I don't embarrass myself with a raging hard-on in a matter of seconds. I turn the swing off and stop it from swaying side to side so I can take my sleeping daughter out. I'm starting to feel more comfortable with her with each passing day. She's not as fragile as I thought she'd be. She can easily hold up her own head. I successfully transfer her into the car seat from the swing, all while keeping her asleep. I snap her in, no longer struggling with the buckle like I did just the other day when I first attempted to place her in the seat.

"Ready?" I ask Riley as I turn in her direction, the car seat already hanging from the crook of my elbow.

"Yep," Riley agrees. "Thank you for dinner," she tells Derek, lifting up on her toes to kiss him on the cheek. He wraps an arm around her, pulling her into a hug.

"Anytime," he tells her before releasing her from his grip. "Don't let this punk give you any shit," he tells her, then flashes a shit-eating grin my way.

"I can hold my own," she tells him, her backbone firmly showing in her confident answer.

"I know you can, still doesn't mean I won't give you some sound advice every once in awhile."

"Okay," she says, and I can see the eye roll she gives him as she moves over to Jillian. They pull each other into a hug.

"See you later this week; don't forget to check the time of that appointment."

"Will do. I'll text you tomorrow, sound good?"

"Sounds perfect. Good night. Love you both," Riley says to Jillian and Derek.

"We love you, too," Jillian tells her as we start walking toward the door. It doesn't take us long to get loaded into my car. I'm getting faster and faster with snapping in the baby seat to the base in my back seat.

We stay quiet on the drive back to my house. The sun has set, so things outside are just illuminated from the lights that line the street. I pull into the driveway, hitting the button to open the garage door. It fully opens by the time I make it up the driveway and am able to pull right into the garage. I sneak a quick glance at Riley as I shut the engine off and can tell that she's tired. I quickly get out of the car and get the car seat from the back seat, carrying Evie inside the house.

I take her straight into the nursery, removing her from the car seat and setting her on the changing pad Riley placed on top of the dresser today. I snag a clean sleeper from one of the drawers below, and a diaper from the bin at the end. She stirs as I start to strip her out of her outfit and is fully awake by the time I get her stripped down. She lets me know just how much she hates being changed when I have the audacity to wipe her with a cold wipe as I change her. "You're just fine," I coo at my daughter. "Daddy's got you," I tell her as I fasten the diaper and then slip the lightweight sleeper on her. It takes me a few seconds to get her arms and legs into it, but thankfully it just zips up, so no buttons for me to fiddle with and ultimately snap together wrong.

"Need any help in here?" Riley asks from the doorway.

"I don't think so. Why don't you head to bed? I'll stay up and give her a bedtime bottle in a little bit. You look like you're exhausted."

"Are you sure? You've got a game tomorrow and need to be well-rested."

"I'm positive. You've been a huge help these last few days, and you're going to have her all by yourself in just a few more when I'm out of town."

"Okay, if you need anything, don't hesitate to wake me up."

"We'll be fine, go to bed, Riley," I tell her, giving her a determined look. I might not know all there is to raising a kid, but I'm damn well going to figure this shit out. I obviously have to rely on someone else to help raise my kid, but I don't want her to ever feel like I wasn't here for her when I could be. Things won't always be like this. There will come a day that I can no longer play the game I grew up loving, and still love with a fiery passion, and I want to be here for my daughter.

With Evie in the crook of one arm, we make our way into the kitchen. I place her in the little bouncy seat contraption that sits on the counter. I make sure that she's buckled in before I step away. I snag one of the bottles and mix it up for her. Another thing I've picked up quickly how to do. I'm slaying this dad shit. With a bottle for Evie and a glass of chocolate milk for me, I collect Evie from the seat and take her out to the living room. I get us settled on the couch and flip the TV on, landing on an old James Bond movie. I only have it on for some background noise as my attention turns to my daughter. I observe her, drinking her in as she lies on the couch between my outstretched legs. She's so content, looking all around. She must see something she likes, as her little legs start kicking in excitement.

"What's got you all excited?" I ask her, my voice taking on an ever-so-slight baby voice. I roll my damn eyes at myself. I must sound like a fucking idiot talking to her. Evie's little arms flail as her legs kick around even move as I speak to her. I wipe a small line of drool from her face, and she grips my finger as I start to pull away. I allow her to keep her grip on my fingers, even though I know she's going to pull them right to her mouth. "You sure create a ton of drool for such a cute baby," I tell her, bopping her on the tip of the nose. She makes a squealing noise that almost sounds like a laugh, but I don't think you can describe what I heard as a laugh just yet.

Evie and I sit here, taking each other in as the time passes. She starts to get fussy about twenty or so minutes later, so I settle her in my arms and offer the bottle. She accepts it immediately and starts sucking it down fast. I hold the bottle, Evie's little hands still gripping my fingers firmly in hers. I watch her as she greedily sucks the formula down. As she nears the end of her bottle, the suckles become almost nonexistent, and her eyes flutter closed. I keep the bottle in place, wanting to make sure that she's asleep before I pull the bottle from her mouth. With the loss of the bottle nipple, she sucks a few times on her tongue before that stops, and she thankfully stays asleep.

I watch her sleeping peacefully in my arms for a little while longer before eventually taking her into the nursery and laying her down in the new crib. She didn't even flinch when I transferred her into it. I make sure nothing is in the crib that could hurt her while sleeping. That was something that Riley schooled me on yesterday when I attempted to place a teddy bear in the crib.

I finally pull myself away from the side of the crib. I'm starting to feel like a creeper on my own daughter. I make sure the baby monitor is on for Riley, and I head out of Evie's room. I shut everything off in the living room, making sure to clean up the few dishes I dirtied, then head for my bedroom. I close the door and immediately pull my T-shirt off over my head. I toss it toward my laundry basket that sits just inside my walk-in closet. My jeans follow the shirt, and I pad into the en-suite bathroom in nothing but my boxer briefs. I take care of business, stopping to wash my hands and brush my teeth before I slide into bed. The coolness of the sheets hitting my skin helps relax me. They don't stay cold for long as my thoughts drift back to the conversation I overheard that was definitely not meant for me to hear. I feel slightly guilty about listening, but not bad enough to have made my presence known. I think it would have embarrassed Riley had she known I was there, hearing what she was telling her sister-in-law. The knowledge that she's a fucking virgin has my cock standing at full salute again.

I slip my hand down my abs until I'm pushing my boxers over my cock and down my hips. I wrap my palm around the base of my cock and give it one long stroke, circling the crown before dropping my palm back down until the edge of my hand hits against my pubic bone. I allow my mind to wander, thinking what it would be like to sink inside her untouched pussy. How fucking tight it must be. I'm not sure she'd be able to take all of me. I'm not saying I've got the biggest cock out there, but I know I'm on the larger size of the ordinary in both length and girth.

"Fuckkk," I moan as my fist moves up and down my shaft, gaining speed as my orgasm builds within my body. I fling the sheets off of me with my free hand and kick my boxers entirely off my body. I don't want to make a mess of them and have to change the sheets before I can go to sleep tonight. Once they're off of my body, I kick them to the bottom of the bed and spread out. My hand works my cock, and before I know what's hit me, my orgasm barrels out of me, hot cum spurting out, covering my abs in my own release.

I suck in a few deep breaths as my body goes limp after the intensity of my release. All the testosterone flooding my system has me ready to pass the fuck out. I allow myself a few moments to bask in the fogginess before I reach over to my bedside table for a few tissues to clean up my stomach. With most of the mess cleaned off of me, I head for the shower to rinse off quickly.

Before sliding back into bed, I right the sheets, finding my boxers balled up within them. I toss them into my laundry basket before I settle into bed for the night. As soon as my head hits the pillow, exhaustion from the day hits me. I make sure my phone is plugged in and roll over, allowing sleep to claim me.

"How was your game?" Riley asks as I drop my bag on the floor and set my wallet, keys, and phone on the counter.

"It was good. We won five to two."

"Awesome. Did Derek pitch tonight?"

"Nope, he wasn't up in the rotation today. He'll be back up later this week. How'd things go around here?" I ask, looking around for any signs of Evie.

"Pretty good. I put Evie down about an hour ago. She was a little fussy this evening. I think she's about to cut that first tooth. I also noticed she was tugging at one of her ears; if that continues, it might be wise to get her in for a check-up. Teething can sometimes cause ear troubles and or an ear infection."

"Will she be okay tonight? Is it something that we need to find a doctor that can see her now?" I ask, starting to panic internally.

"She should be fine tonight, no need for an emergency room. If I notice she's still tugging at it tomorrow morning, we can call her pediatrician and get her in. Did Erica leave you any information on who that is?" she asks.

"I think that information was in the diaper bag. Maybe on the shot record card?" I tell her, trying to remember what information I do have. Erica didn't leave much, that's for damn sure.

"I'll look through everything and see if I can figure it out. If not, I'm sure Jillian can get us the name of the doctor that she takes the girls to and see if they can get Evie in for a new patient appointment."

"Whatever works. Even if we do find out who Erica took her to, if they're located far away, it might make more sense to move her to the office Jillian takes the girls to anyways," I suggest.

"That's true. I'll look tonight before I go to bed, and you can make that decision in the morning," Riley says.

"Sounds good." I pick my bag back up and turn to take it to my room. I empty the few things out of it, putting them away before I strip out of the clothes I wore home from the game. Unlike some professional sports like hockey, we're not required to dress in a suit going and coming from games. I'd hate that shit, not that I don't dress nicely, but not suit and tie nice day in and day out.

I slip on some clean sweats, forgoing a shirt, as I make my way back out to the living room. Riley has moved from the kitchen to the living room. I have a few seconds to take her in, curled up on my couch as she watches TV. Her hair is piled on top of her head in a messy bun; she's got an oversized hoodie sweatshirt paired with a pair of way to fucking short shorts. They show off her legs and tight ass.

"Whatcha watching?" I ask, taking a seat on the opposite end of the couch.

"Nothing specific, I was just scrolling through the options," she tells me, tossing the remote to me. "Not much is on tonight."

"That's the problem with the spring and summer months. All the regular shows have ended, but none of the summer shows have started yet."

"Yep," she agrees with me quickly. I leave the TV on the channel she'd stopped on. I flick my eyes to the screen and watch as some contestants on the cooking show all plate their food for the judges. I only keep them there for a few seconds before my eyes back on Riley, or as much of it as I can without her thinking I'm a creeper or some shit like that. I watch her from my peripheral vision and take notice as she relaxes into the couch just a little bit more.

I shift on the couch so I can take her in easier. Her natural beauty about knocks me on my ass. The gentle curve of her neck, the way she's got her hair piled up on the top of her head in a messy bun, makes me want to reach out and tug that band out of it, allowing it to cascade down her back. I'd run my fingers through it, wrapping it around my fist as I took a handful, allowing me to guide her right where I want her. I can envision reaching up and grabbing a fistful as I slide into her from behind. That thought has my cock hardening in my sweats, hard enough that I'm going to be tenting them any second now if I'm not careful. I reach over to the chair and snag the throw pillow off of it and place it on my lap, so I don't scare the poor girl with what she does to me.

"Before time gets away from us, can we go over your schedule?" Riley asks, pulling me out of my daydreaming about fucking her. "I want to make sure I have everything on my calendar."

I clear my throat, knowing that if I don't, it will more than likely give away that my mind was not in the present. "Yeah, sure," I tell her, grabbing my phone. I watch as Riley stands and heads into the kitchen, returning with a calendar, pen, and her phone.

"I picked up a planner, plus will put things into my phone, that way, I can easily see when you'll be here and gone," she says, sitting back down on the couch, this time with her legs crossed and facing me. She opens the planner to the current month and pulls out a few colored pens from a package I didn't notice at first.

"Color coding things?" I ask.

"Yep. I love planners and making them look cute," she tells me, flashing the sweetest smile that has my heart fluttering a thousand beats a minute.

"All right. Do you want me to go day by day? Start with practices? Home games? Road trips? You tell me how you want to do this."

"Ummm... hold on, I'll be right back," she says, setting everything down as she jumps up and disappears down the hall, returning this time with a notebook of paper. She sits back down, legs once again folded like they were before, and facing me. "Okay, start with tomorrow, and I'll write everything down, then I can transfer it all to my planner once I figure out my color-coordinating plan."

I chuckle at her excitement over organizing my schedule. "Okay, crazy girl," I say, shaking my head as I laugh at her. I open my calendar app and start rattling off my schedule for the next few weeks to her. Since we're doing this as a trial run for the next few weeks, we only go over that amount of time, for now.

"Okay, I'll use red for when you'll be out of town, that way those days stick out to me as being the entire time, home games in blue and home practices in green," she murmurs as she marks things down in her notebook.

I watch as she starts to write things in her actual planner, marking everything down in one color before she moves to the next. "All right, all done!" she says about ten minutes later. She holds up the planner and shows it to me. The smile that lights up her face shows me just how proud of herself she is, and it's adorable.

"Seeing it like that makes me tired just thinking about it."

"It is quite a crazy schedule. I always wondered how Derek kept up with it when he first went pro. Now when I see it written out like this, it makes me think that the wives and girlfriends almost have it worse. Lots of times during the season that they're practically single parents."

"I never thought of it that way," I tell her honestly. My focus has always been on the game first and partying second. Each city we visit, I know all the hot spots to hit up after our games if we're not wheels up right away. Those places are usually crawling with cleat chasers, ones that I've definitely taken what they've been offering in the past without a care in the world. Funny how a kid being dropped on your doorstep has you second-guessing partaking in that kind of thing again. "I know this arrangement is asking a lot of you, so thank you again for stepping in to help me out. I'd seriously be lost without you."

"I'm happy to help," she says, the honesty in her words evident, especially in the way that she looks at me. She sets the planner and pens down on the coffee table and looks back at me. "I wouldn't be here if I didn't want to be," she says, sucking her bottom lip in between her teeth, biting it slightly before releasing it. "Plus, that little girl in there has already gotten her little hands around my heart and pulled me in. She's kind of addicting," she tells me as a smile breaks out on those lips. Lips that would be so easy to lean forward and capture with my own.

"She is pretty damn cute," I muse, agreeing with her about my daughter. "She's grabbed me by the heart, as well," I confess.

"You're doing a great job with her so far," Riley assures me.

"You think so?"

"Absolutely. You're going to be a great dad, Justin. Don't let anyone tell you anything different."

"Thanks," I tell her as we make eye contact. I see something flash in her eyes just as I feel the air between us shift. She sucks that damn lip back between her teeth, and my eyes drop and focus in on where her teeth are biting hard on her lip. Before I know what I'm even doing, I reach out and slowly slide my thumb along her lip, pulling it from her teeth. "You bite any harder, and you're going to break the skin," I tell her, my words coming out gruffly. I clear my throat, attempting to remove the grit away before I continue. "You keep it up, and I'll have to kiss it all better."

I flick my eyes back up to hers and watch as her pupils dilate. She wants me just as bad as I want her, I can see it. I watch as her eyes drop ever so slightly to my lips. My tongue darts out, wetting my lips, and her eyes track it as I do so. I can't help from smirking at how zoned in she is on my every movement.

I slide my full hand along her cheek and back until I'm cupping her neck. I pull her forward as I move in her direction at that same time, closing the distance between the two of us. Once we're a hairs breadth apart, I bring my other hand up to cup her cheek, swiping my thumb across her bottom lip once again. "Tell me to stop if you don't want me to kiss you, Riley," I whisper between the two of us. I give her a few seconds to tell me no or to stop before I cover her lips with my own. I don't go in full force; I ease into this kiss. Her lips taste like berries and are the softest lips mine have ever kissed. I pull her closer until she's on my lap. My hands sink into that hair, allowing me to angle her head so I can deepen the kiss. I swipe my tongue along the seam of her lips, and she opens for me. I lick my way inside her mouth. The moment our tongues collide, I swear fucking fireworks start to explode.

We finally break the kiss, both sucking in lungs full of air. Riley drops her forehead to my shoulder, her hands resting against my bare abs. I feel her tense in my lap at the same moment her fingers still from tracing the ridges of my abs. She pulls back, sitting up straight and moving off of my lap and standing up quickly. She almost trips over my feet, so I reach out, grasping her hips to help steady her. I don't need her falling and getting hurt.

"Riley," I say her name. It comes out in a half growl, half plea. "Look at me, please," I ask, tugging on her hand. She sucks in a deep breath before turning around to face me. I can see the confused look on her face. The one that tells me she wants more but also is confused about what just happened between the two of us. "Talk to me."

"Wh-what are we doing? That can't happen again, JJ," she whispers, and brings her other hand up until her fingertips rest on her lips. I can still feel her lips against my own, so I can only imagine that she feels mine.

"We were being two consenting adults exploring this spark between the two of us. One that I'm pretty sure you can feel just as much as I can."

"We can't," she states, not very convincingly.

"Why not?"

"For so many reasons, JJ," she tells me, pulling her hand from my grip. "You're my brother's best friend. Your life just got turned upside down. You don't *do* relationships, and I'm not about to indulge in a one-night stand. And most of all, you're my boss, JJ. We just can't."

Before I can reply, Riley pivots and runs from the room. I sit there a bit stunned, a bit pissed, but most of all I'm fired up. I'm ready to toss all of Riley's reasons out the fucking door and show her that if there's something real between the two of us, that none of those reasons matter and we can make something work if it's meant to be.

Game fucking on.

TEN
RILEY

I CLOSE THE DOOR TO MY BEDROOM, FLICKING THE LOCK on the knob. Not because I think that JJ will try and come in here after me, but because I'm afraid that I'll run right back out into the living room and tell him to take me to bed right now. I can't believe that he kissed me just now. The feel of his lips against my own, the way his hands caressed my skin was more than I could have ever thought that it could be like. I've only ever dreamed of being kissed like that by a man. The few guys I've kissed and made out with were nowhere near as experienced as JJ was just now.

The reality as to *why* JJ was so much more experienced hits me like a bucket of ice water. He's a manwhore to the core. Hell, the night that Derek and I came over here when Evie was dropped off, he'd been initially on his way out to go party it up, and I'm sure that one of the things he'd planned to do that night was find some random chick to fuck.

I scrub my hands over my face and groan into them.

Why didn't I tell him no or to stop when he gave me the out? I think I was just so shell-shocked that he was touching me, seeing me in that kind of light, that I just froze. When he walked back out without a shirt on, I'm surprised my chin didn't literally hit the floor. The man has more abs than I knew existed, and my traitorous mind went right to what it would be like to trace all those ridges with my tongue. What it would feel like to have all that skin against my own.

It's not fair, really. I'm so sexually frustrated, and I'm trapped in this house with a god of a man. One that I can't touch. I push away from the door and head for the bathroom. If I can't give in to my desires with JJ, I can for sure use that kiss as fodder to get myself off in the bath.

I plug the tub and start filling it, grabbing some bath salts from my toiletries bag. They were part of a gift set that Jillian and Derek got me for Christmas. I add the salts to the water and then grab a towel from the closet. Before I slide into the water, I go back into the room and grab my vibrator from the bedside drawer that I stashed it in. I might not have ever had sex with a man, but that doesn't mean I've never taken care of myself. I'm twenty-two for Christ's sake. There's no real reason behind the fact that I'm still a virgin. I haven't been saving myself for marriage or anything like that. It just hasn't happened. I never had a serious boyfriend that I felt like we were ready to take that step. I've done my fair share of fooling around, but I've never had sex or had a guy go down on me. I've given my fair share of blow jobs, but that's the extent of my sexual experience.

I grab the baby monitor, making sure it is turned on, but at the lowest setting. I set it on the counter where I can still see it from the bath, then turn on some music on my phone. I slip into the hot water and feel my muscles relax as I sit back. The bath salts add a very calming scent to the air, helping me to relax even more. I lay my head back, closing my eyes, and sink another inch down in the water. My mind goes right back to the couch, and that kiss. My pulse kicks right back up as my center clenches. There was no avoiding just how hard Justin was underneath me, and I'm not talking about his abs. He was definitely aroused and hard in his sweats. The thought that I did that to him makes me pause for a second. The fact that he'd possibly want me is baffling. He can have any woman he wants, probably has had every woman he's ever wanted, yet he kissed me tonight and was hard for *me*.

I cup my breasts, rolling my nipples before one of my hands slides down my body. I circle my clit with my fingertips, wishing like hell that it were JJ touching me. My body is still strung tight from our short make-out session. I grab my vibrator from the edge of the tub and bring it down to my entrance. I turn it on the first setting and slide it inside my pussy. The vibrations are a welcome intrusion. I increase the intensity as I slide it in deeper. It hits my g-spot at the same time as the external vibrations hit my clit. With both areas being stimulated at the same time, I come hard. My body convulses around the toy, and I bite my lip to keep from yelling out as I come.

I pull the vibrator from my body, having to concentrate hard to turn it off before I set it back on the edge of the tub. I sit back once again letting the hot water relax me even further, hoping that once I get out of the water, I'll be able to fall asleep.

The water starts to turn cold, so I pull the plug and climb out as it drains. I wrap the fluffy towel around my sated body. The towel bar is heated, so my towel is warm and feels like heaven. I dry completely off then grab my favorite lotion to apply everywhere. Once I'm fully lotioned up, I scrub my face and brush my teeth before heading back into the bedroom. I pull on some sleep shorts and a tank top, my usual bedtime uniform.

The hotness from the tub catches up to me, making me really want a glass of ice water to cool off before I fall asleep. I stand here in the room, wondering if I should risk going back out there. I really don't want to run into JJ tonight. Not after what I just ran from.

I stand with my ear pressed against the door, trying to listen for any noises coming from the living room. After a minute or so of not hearing anything, I slowly open the door as quietly as possible, looking down the hall. The coast appears to be clear, as the house is dark. I silently pad down the hall and into the kitchen. I grab my water bottle from the counter and open the freezer to grab a handful of ice to place in it. I don't want the noise of the ice maker going off to alert JJ of my presence. I quickly add the ice and then close the door and just about jump out of my clothes when I see JJ standing at the doorway, leaning against the frame as he takes me in.

"Fuck, you scared me!" I yelp, smacking my hand against my chest and about dropping my water bottle.

"Sorry," he says, not that I believe him one bit. The

desire that is written all over his face is unmistakable, even in the darkness. The only light that fills the room is the small night light coming from the few under-cabinet lights that get left on overnight.

I go back to filling my water bottle up, then secure the lid once it's full. "Just needed some water before bed," I finally tell him, attempting to break the awkward silence.

"Did you have a relaxing bath?" he asks, a smirk still painting his lips.

"Ho-how did you know I took a bath?" I ask, confused about his knowledge of what I did. The thought hits me about everything that I did in that tub and can feel my cheeks heat in a blush. Does he know I made myself come thinking about him?

"I could hear the water running," he says, and I blow out a huge breath.

"Oh," I say, so quietly, I'm not even sure if he could hear me with the distance that is still between us. "It was relaxing," I finally tell him, realizing I never answered his question.

"I'm glad. You were a little tense, there, before you went into your room," he says, bringing my attention back to that moment.

I don't know what to say, so I just nod my head up and down as I stare in his direction. I can feel the heat start to leave my cheeks. Before either one of us can say anything else, Evie cries out, saving me from this awkward moment. "I'd better go get her," I say, escaping past JJ and down the hall.

I enter Evie's room, heading straight for the crib. I pick

her up, soothing her as I attempt to soothe myself. My heart is beating fast after that encounter with JJ in the kitchen. I don't know what's going to happen between the two of us, but I can't deal with any of that right now. Right now, this little girl needs my attention.

I lay her down on the changing table and quickly take care of her wet diaper. She feels a little warm to the touch, so once I've got her zipped back into her sleeper, I snag the thermometer from one of the bins on the table and swipe it over her forehead. As I figured, she's running a little warm, so I grab the baby Tylenol and bring it with me out to the kitchen. JJ has retreated to the living room where he's sitting on the couch watching something on TV, sounds like some sports channel recapping things that happened today in the sports world.

I make quick work of mixing up a bottle for Miss Evie. Once it is ready, I take it, along with the medicine, and head for the living room. I sit down on one of the recliner chairs, placing Evie, so she's facing me, propped up on my legs. She's not fussing right now as she looks around the room. That gives me the chance to read the bottle of medicine so I can see how much she needs. I open the package and measure it out, I lightly pinch her lips, making it look like she's got fish lips, then squirt it into her mouth, aiming for her cheek.

"What are you doing?" JJ asks.

"She's running a low-grade fever, so I'm giving her something for it," I tell him.

"What was that with her face?"

"Oh, just a trick to getting the medicine in her mouth

and actually down. If she'd spit it out, it would have made a mess, but also, then it is hard to determine if she actually got any and, if so, how much. You have to be careful not to overdose a baby with this stuff. With a small body, too much Tylenol at once can cause damage to her kidneys."

"Good to know," he states. "So, you just pinch her cheeks?"

"Basically. Just make them look like fish lips," I explain, stopping and showing him with my own. "Then you can slip the little dropper into her mouth and squirt it into the cheek. If you squirt it straight back, you risk it hitting her gag reflex or her choking on it."

"I would have never known any of that," he says, scrubbing a hand down his face.

"You'll get there," I remind him. "You have to remember that I've been babysitting for years. I've had a lot of time to learn all these things."

"Yeah," he half-heartedly agrees with me. "I'm guessing that with the fever, we'll need to call the doctor in the morning?"

"Yeah, I'm still leaning toward the culprit being the teething, but she could have an ear infection, as well. Doesn't hurt to get her checked out."

"Okay. Is that something that you can take care of, or do I need to make the call?" he asks.

"I can call, but you'll probably have to go with us, at least this first time. You should be able to give them permission to release her information to me. You'll probably also have to add me to an approved list of adults that can seek medical attention for her. Since I'm not her mother, I don't have any legal right to do so."

"That's understandable. If you can call in the morning, first thing, I can make sure to be available."

"I'll do that and then let you know when the appointment is. Once she's down, I'll look for that paperwork to see what office Erica was taking her to."

"Thanks, Riley."

"You're welcome, JJ," I tell him as I offer Evie the bottle that I made for her. "I'll let you know as soon as I have an appointment scheduled for her. On second thought, does morning or afternoon work best, if I'm given a choice?"

"I can be flexible; Coach will let me out of practice for this tomorrow without any issues. He's aware of what is going on, and I've been assured that I have the full support from the team and front office for whatever I need during this transition time."

"Okay, sounds good. I'll hopefully know first thing," I tell him as Evie spits the nipple of the bottle out of her mouth. She starts to fuss, so I shift her until she's lying on my chest. I alternate between patting her back and rubbing it. I can tell she doesn't feel right, and she didn't drink much of the bottle, so I don't really think it's an air bubble trapped. She settles against my chest; I'm sure the sound of my heartbeat soothing to her little ears.

"How'd you do that?" JJ asks, pointing to Evie on my chest. The bewildered look on his face has me melting just a little bit more for him. He's so out of his element with this cute little girl that it's almost comical at times.

"Babies are so used to hearing their mother's heartbeat

while in utero that the sound is calming to them. It doesn't have to just be the mom's, that's why you'll see parents doing skin-to-skin with a baby on their chest. Not only does your body temperature help regulate hers, but the sound of your heart will soothe her, as well."

"I would have never known that."

"You can't learn everything in one day, JJ. Just give it some time. I know this is all probably very overwhelming, but I promise that you'll get through all of it."

"If you say so," he deadpans.

"I think I'm going to go put her down and see if I can find that paperwork, then get some sleep while I can. I have a feeling she might be up throughout the night tonight. What time do you plan to leave in the morning?" I ask a few minutes later.

"Not until around ten, unless we need to be at the doctor's then."

"Most offices open between seven thirty and eight, so we should definitely know by then what time we can take her in."

"Sounds good. If you need anything during the night, don't hesitate to come get me. I don't expect you to do everything."

"I know," I tell him, flashing him a quick smile, hoping that I don't reveal that I have no plans to wake him up for help.

I take Evie to my room and place her in the pack-n-play to sleep. I'd rather have her close by than in the nursery. Thankfully, I'm able to transfer her successfully without her waking up. She's still warm to the touch, so hopefully, the medicine kicks in soon and helps take that fever down. I grab the thermometer and baby Tylenol and stash it in the side pocket of the pack-n-play so I can easily find it in the middle of the night if needed.

I dig through the little bit of paperwork that Erica left and, thankfully, found the doctor's information that saw her when she was first born, and again for the necessary checkups she's already had. I leave the papers out so that it is easily accessible first thing in the morning for me to call. I pull the clinic up on my phone and realize that it is a clinic not far away and might just be the same one that Jillian takes the girls to.

I quickly brush my teeth and use the bathroom before I'm sliding between the crisp sheets. I hardly get a couple of pages of my book read before I can't keep my eyes open and allow sleep to claim me.

I startle awake, feeling like I fell asleep just a few minutes ago, but realize that it's the alarm on my phone waking me up. I look around and see Evie sleeping right where I left her last night. I'm shocked that she's still asleep and jump from the bed to make sure that she's still breathing. Upon closer inspection, she's perfectly fine, breathing like usual. I gently touch the back of my fingers against her cheek and then forehead to check on her fever, and unfortunately, she's once again warm to the touch. I snag the thermometer out of the side pocket the pack-n-play and scan it across her forehead. She's a half-degree or so higher than she was last night, so I go ahead and ready another dose to give her once she's awake.

Since she's still asleep, I grab the paperwork I set out

last night, taking it back over to my bed. I pull my cell out and dial the number. I take both the paper and my phone out of my room as I don't want to wake Evie up while talking on the phone. I pad out to the kitchen, my phone to my ear as it starts ringing.

Thankfully, it doesn't take long to reach a receptionist, and they're able to get us in to see the doctor in just over an hour. Once I'm off the phone, I flip the coffee pot on, turning to head back to my room. Except, when I turn around, my ovaries about explode as I find a shirtless JJ holding Evie in his arms. Her cheeks are all rosy from the fever. She just looks miserable and like she doesn't feel right. "Morning," I say just above a whisper.

"Morning," JJ replies, his voice still deep, gravely, and sleep-filled. My mind quickly dips into the gutter with thoughts of what his voice would sound like if woken up with some morning sex. I promptly shake that thought from my mind. I need to concentrate on Evie and not JJ and sex.

"I've already talked to the doctor's office, and we have an appointment at nine fifteen."

"Sounds good," he says, his eyes flicking over to the clock. "It looks like we've got to get ready then."

"Yep," I tell him. "Want me to take her so you can go do just that?"

"I can keep her while you get ready," he says, walking over to start a bottle for her.

"Are you sure? I just need to toss on some clean clothes."

"Yep, I'm good. Go get ready. I'll drink some coffee and

give Evie, here, her bottle," he assures me as he starts shaking the bottle up to mix it.

I take two more seconds to observe him with his daughter before I run down the hall and into my bedroom. It should be illegal how good the man looks with a baby in his arms. He might not have ever thought of himself as a family man, but that guy is a natural. Before he knows it, he'll be a full-fledged, proud card-carrying member of the girl dad tribe.

I head for the bathroom and take care of business, then run a brush through my hair before I pull it up into a pony-tail. I pull out a pair of shorts, a tank top, and sandals. Within ten minutes, I'm fully dressed and ready for the day, so I head back out to the kitchen, where I find JJ sitting at the table with Evie sucking down her bottle.

"Want me to take her so you can go get ready now?" I offer as I grab a mug and fill it with coffee, adding creamer to the top.

"Maybe in a minute or so. I'll let her finish the bottle," he tells me.

"Did you want to take separate cars so that you can leave from the appointment and go straight to practice?" I ask.

"That's okay; I can drive the two of you there. Like I said last night, Coach won't have any issues if I have to sit today out. I already shot him a text that I've got to take her to the doctor this morning and I didn't know if I'd be there. I don't want to miss anything they tell us."

"Okay."

ELEVEN
JUSTIN

I watch Riley from across the kitchen as she sips from her coffee cup. She looks so relaxed, but also sexy as hell in her shorts and tank top. It might just be my favorite shirt of hers that she's worn around me so far. It's cut just low enough to show off the very top swells of her breasts, but not so much cleavage that it is trashy or off-putting. The way that her waist nips in and her hips flare out have some dirty thoughts running a constant loop in my mind of how they'd be the perfect place for me to hold on while I pound into her from behind. Her ass looks like it would make the ideal place to grip or spank while I'm balls deep, as well.

"JJ!" Riley says my name, snapping her fingers not far from my face. "Did you hear me?" I look up at her, standing just in front of me now instead of across the room where she just was a few seconds ago.

"Yeah, sorry. I zoned out there for a few seconds. What were you saying?"

"You should probably go get ready, we need to leave soon."

"Right," I tell her, standing up and grabbing my coffee cup to take to the sink. "Here, can you take her?" I ask, holding up a sleepy Evie to her. She easily transfers Evie to her arms, making sure she's settled nicely. I look down at my daughter, sleeping peacefully against Riley's chest, and I can't believe it, but I'm fucking jealous of my own daughter. Her head is centered right between Riley's breasts, Evie's ear is against Riley's chest, and I'm sure she's listening to her heartbeat as she sleeps there so peacefully.

I force myself to turn away from the two of them, heading for my bedroom. I drop the shorts I pulled on when I got up this morning, heading straight for the shower. I've had a permanent hard-on since Riley has been around, and this morning is no different.

I flip on the shower, leaving the temperature on the cold side. It doesn't really do much for my situation, it just makes me fucking cold, so before long I crank it up until it's almost scalding. I lather the soap on my chest, making sure not to miss an inch of my skin. As I make my way down my body, my cock stirs once again, and with a soap-covered hand, I slide my palm down my shaft. It hardens at the friction as my palm slides from the root to the tip. I give myself a few pulls before I move on to wash the rest of my body. Once I'm all rinsed off, my cock is still begging for a release, so I plant my right hand against the wall and allow my left to stroke up and down my shaft. I circle around the head, giving it a little extra tug. Thoughts of Riley flood my mind. She's all that fills my spank bank these days. That kiss from last night is filling a good part of my fodder. I think about what her lips felt like. How pillowy soft they were. How perfect it felt to be kissing her and have her body pressed up against mine. When our lips collided, it was like an axis inside me shifted that I never knew wasn't aligned correctly.

I can feel my orgasm starting to tingle at the base of my spine, so I increase the speed of my strokes. My head falls forward and I think of licking Riley's pussy, bringing her to an orgasm as my own releases, spraying on the tile wall of my shower. I stroke myself through my orgasm, letting my body empty all of it. I'm sated and spent, but know I can't slack off. We've got to get going soon, so I grab the removable shower head and spray the wall, washing away the mess I just made. I quickly finish up before shutting the water off and getting out. Once I'm toweled off, I head for my closet. I pull on a clean pair of boxer briefs, then a pair of shorts and a T-shirt. I quickly run a comb through my hair then toss on my baseball hat.

I slip into some sandals and then head back out to the kitchen, where I find Riley placing Evie in her car seat. The diaper bag is sitting next to her, looking like it's already been packed for our morning outing. "Need any help?" I offer a few seconds later.

"I think we're all good," Riley states, looking up at me for a split second before her focus returns to Evie and getting her ready for us to leave.

"Here," I say once Evie is buckled, but before Riley can pick the seat up. "Let me carry her. You can grab the diaper bag," I say.

"Sure."

We both head for the garage door, I stop to hold the door open for Riley. I reach over and snatch my keys and wallet off the table once she's passed through. I slip my wallet in my back pocket then pat all of my other ones to make sure I have my phone with me. Once satisfied that I have everything that I need, I secure Evie into the back seat, snapping her car seat into the base like I've done it a time or two now.

Once in the driver's seat, Riley gives me the address of where we're going so I can plug it into my GPS. Once that populates on the screen, we're off to the appointment.

It takes maybe ten minutes to get to the doctor's office. Before we get out of the car, I pull my baseball hat down just a tad bit lower on my head. I hope no one recognizes me while we're here. The last thing I need is someone snapping a picture of me with Evie and leaking it to the press. So far, I haven't received any messages about anything being leaked yet, but I'm sure it's just a matter of time. Lucas should be working on that press release for me, hopefully today.

We enter the doctor's office and head straight for the receptionist's desk. I hand over my insurance card, realizing that I haven't yet had Evie added to my insurance. The front desk lady assures me that it is okay, and they can put the information on file and get things sent to them in a few days, once I can get her added. I never even thought of that until now. I make sure to add Riley, along with my parents and Jillian, as people who can have access to Evie's medical records. Erica had already listed me on the paperwork as her father, so that wasn't an issue, at least.

With all the paperwork taken care of, I follow Riley to an open seat. Thankfully, it is tucked away from the main entrance and allows me to be out of the main view as people enter and exit. I pull my phone from my pocket as we wait and shoot off a quick text to Derek, asking him if he can stop into the team's office and ask what I need to add Evie to my insurance. I'm sure there's some kind of paperwork that I'll need to fill out, and maybe they'll give it to him to bring to me.

"Evelyn." A nurse calls out my daughter's name from an open doorway. Riley and I both stand and I grab the baby carrier and head towards the nurse. I know the moment she recognizes me, as her eyes go all big like saucers, but she quickly recovers as we reach her. "Right this way," she says, a blush flushing her cheeks.

"Thanks," Riley tells her as we follow her down a hall-way. We stop at an alcove that has a scale and a measure-ment device on the wall to measure kids' heights.

"We need to get Evelyn's weight and length, can you please take her out of the seat and strip her down to her diaper?" the nurse asks. I watch as she takes out a paper sheet and places it on a device on the counter.

Thankfully, Riley is with me as she's already taken Evie from her seat and has laid her down and is starting to remove her clothes.

"Why do you need her stripped-down?" I ask.

"We need to be as accurate as we can get for her weight. So many medications are based on weight, and if we have a couple of pounds of clothes in the way, it could cause the doctor to miss-dose her, and we wouldn't want that," she tells us as she writes down what the screen says. "You can re-dress her now," she tells Riley once she's got the info she needed.

Once Evie is back in her sleeper, the nurse stretches her legs out and marks the paper sheet with her pen, both at her head and where the bottom of her foot reaches. "You can pick her up now," she says, and I step in and pick Evie up. She's stayed calm through all of this so far, and I'd like to keep it that way. I watch as the nurse pulls out a small tape measure and stretches it out between the two marks she made on the paper then note that on her note pad. "Follow me, and we'll get you guys into a room."

We do just that and follow her into an exam room just around the corner. "What brings you in today?" she asks.

"Evie's been running a fever since last night. I noticed she was also tugging at her ear yesterday before the fever started, and she's just been a little cranky the last twenty-four hours," Riley tells her.

"Poor girl," the nurse says, pulling her stethoscope out of a pocket. "Mind if I listen?" she asks, and I shift Evie so that she can access her chest. We stay quiet while she listens to her. "Any other symptoms?" the nurse asks, writing down a few more things on her pad.

"She's been chewing on everything, so we weren't sure if this all was related to her maybe teething," I speak up for the first time since we entered the room.

"That's definitely a possibility. Let me get all these notes entered into the system, and the doctor will be with you in just a few minutes."

"Thank you," Riley and I both tell the nurse as she exits the room.

"She recognized you," Riley says just above a whisper once the door latches. "Do you think that will be a problem?"

"You picked up on that, did you?" I ask, a little shocked she noticed, too.

"I did, but she recovered quickly."

"She did," I say as Evie starts to fuss a little bit in my arms. I shift her, so she's lying on my chest rather than having her back to my front. Riley hands me the bottle she made and tucked into the diaper bag. I shift Evie once again, offering her the bottle that she accepts quickly. "I'd hope that she wouldn't say anything to anyone about me being in here with my daughter. That would be quite the HIPPA violation."

"You're right about that. I don't think you'll have an issue. Jillian texted me this morning that this is the office that they bring the girls, and they've never had an issue with them leaking anything," Riley says, reassuring me that we'll be okay here.

"Knock, knock," a voice rings out as the door slowly swings open. A youngish doctor steps through the doorway, looking at Riley and then myself. If he recognizes me, he hides it well. "Hello, I'm Dr. Shane, I hear Miss Evelyn isn't feeling well," he says as he heads straight for the small sink and washes his hands.

Once he dries his hands, he motions to the exam table. "Do you mind laying her down up here?"

"Oh, of course," I say, taking the bottle from Evie and placing her in the middle of the table.

I stand close by as he listens to her, then checks her ears, nose, and mouth.

"She definitely has an ear infection going on, so I'll call in some antibiotics for that. Her gums are a little swollen, so your assumption that she might be teething is probably correct. Once the tooth breaks the skin, things should get a little better, but she might also start pushing through a few at a time, thus stretching out that time that things will bother her. Tylenol, as needed to help with the pain and or fevers that can come along with it, is perfectly fine, but if you notice the ear tugging again, bring her back in so we can take a look at the ears."

"Did you get all of that?" I ask Riley.

"Yes," she says, a little chuckle escaping as she gives me an inquisitive look. "Did *you* get all of that?" she throws my question back at me.

"Not really," I tell her honestly. I turn back to Dr. Shane. "I just want to make sure that if Riley has to bring Evie in for any reason when I'm gone for work that she won't have any issues doing so."

"As long as she's been listed as an approved person to seek treatment and receive information, then you'll be all set," he assures me.

"Okay, just making sure," I tell him. "I have to head out of town this week and don't want there to be any issues if something was to arise, and they needed to come back."

"I'll make an additional note in her chart, but you should be all set with the signed release."

"Thanks. It's been quite the whirlwind of a week since I even found out about her, so this is all new territory for me, Doc," I find myself rambling to him.

"I'll have to admit, I was a little shocked to walk in here today and find the two of you with Evelyn and not Erica," he tells us.

"Yeah." I blow out a breath, take off my hat, and run my fingers through my hair before I put it back on. "She showed up on my doorstep last week saying that Evie was mine and that she couldn't do it anymore, and left. We had a paternity test done as quickly as possible, and thankfully my friends stepped in right away to help me out," I tell him.

"That's good. I'm guessing you have things set up for while you're gone on the road, then?" he says, motioning to Riley.

"Yeah. Riley, here, is Evie's nanny. She's a family friend, so I know I can trust her with my girl."

"Support, especially with an infant, is important. Our office is always just a phone call away, if needed. Even in the middle of the night or on the weekends, you can call after hours and our answering service will page the on-call doctor to call you back. We also have evening and weekend appointments for sick visits, so just keep that in mind for the future."

"Thank you, Dr. Shane," I tell him, offering my hand for him to shake. Evie starts to fuss again, so I scoop her up into my arms.

"You're welcome. I'll get that script sent to the phar-macy indicated in the computer when you checked in," he indicates as he heads for the door. "Any other questions before I head out?" he asks.

I look over at Riley, to see if she has anything, before I speak up again.

"I'm good," she states to both of us.

"Doesn't sound like it, Doc. Thanks again for your help."

"Anytime, that's what I'm here for," he says reassuringly. "You can head right out, no need to stop at the front desk to check out."

"Thanks," I call out to his retreating back. Riley takes Evie from me and starts getting her strapped into the seat, and a few minutes later, we're making our way out of the office.

"I'm glad we got that out of the way," I tell Riley once we're all buckled into the car. "He seemed nice," I add.

"I agree. He knew his stuff and was efficient," she says as she shifts in the passenger seat. "Did you want to stop at the pharmacy on the way back home, or I can run out in a little while and pick it up?"

"We can stop there and see how long it will be. I'll probably have to pay cash for it today since she isn't on my insurance yet."

"You're probably right," she agrees with me.

I pull out of the parking lot and head for the pharmacy. Thankfully, it doesn't take long after we arrive for them to have the prescription ready.

"Do you want to practice giving it to her?" Riley asks once we're home and settled into the living room.

"I guess," I tell her, a little nervous about it, if I'm honest.

"It isn't hard, I promise."

"That's what she said." I try and crack a joke to lighten my anxiety.

"You didn't just say that!" Riley barks out a laugh, and her entire face lights up.

"I did," I confess, hanging my head in mock shame, and she giggles at my antics. I'd do it all again to get that sound to come from her lips. "Okay, walk me through this again," I tell her, getting back to the topic at hand.

"Measure out the medicine. I always say to read the dosage instructions each time so that you don't ever mess them up," she suggests. I read the label then stick the syringe tip into the stopper the pharmacy put into the bottle to make it easier to dispense the medicine. I pull the plunger part and fill the syringe to the correct dosage, then flip the bottle back over and pull the tip from the bottle.

"Okay, I've got it ready," I tell her as she shifts Evie on her lap.

"Now, pinch her cheeks lightly, put the syringe in her mouth, angling it towards her cheek, and then squirt it all in her mouth."

I do as she instructs, thankfully getting it all in her mouth on the first try. "That was great," Riley tells me, patting me on the back once I've finished.

"Thanks," I tell her as I step back. I take the medicine and syringe into the kitchen. The meds have to be kept in the fridge, so I place the bottle in there and wash out the syringe.

"I've got everything under control here if you want to head in to practice," Riley tells me when I rejoin them in the living room.

"I probably should," I admit. I pull off my ball cap and run my fingers through my hair a few times before pulling it back down. "I'll be back later," I tell her as I bend down and place a kiss on the top of Evie's head. This brings me incredibly close to Riley's lips, and I find myself wanting to kiss her again. All I can think of at this moment is what it was like to have her lips locked with my own. My eyes flick to hers, and I can see the same desires in her eyes. I push away quickly before I can say fuck it and take her mouth with my own.

I take off to my bedroom, grab my bag, and head out the door like I'm being chased.

TWELVE
RILEY

I carry Evie outside in the backyard, sitting her down on a blanket I've spread out on the grass. Summer has fully arrived in Indianapolis now that we're well into June. My first few months working for JJ and taking care of this precious little girl flew by. We've found a sound system that works for all of us. When his schedule allows, I take one day off per week. I usually end up still staying here at his house, since it's a pain to pack up what I need for just one night at Derek's old condo. But it is nice to have a day that I know I'm not required or on call and can just do whatever I want.

Evie sits on the blanket, shaking one of her toys. She seems so big now, at just over six months old. It looks like she's doing something new every day. She just mastered the unassisted sitting milestone in the past couple of days, and I can't wait for JJ to see it in person. I sent him a few video clips of her doing it, since he's on the road for a couple of games. He's scheduled to get home late tonight, they had an early game today and then he'll fly home once it ends.

"Evie, baby. Who's a big girl?" I ask her, grabbing her attention as I lay on the blanket a foot or so away from her. I pick up one of the toys and shake it for her, getting a shriek of excitement as she shakes her hands faster and babbles. The toy she's got in her hands goes into her mouth. She's teething yet again, already working on her third tooth. Girlfriend has been a teething mess since she was three months old.

"Auntie RyRy!" I hear my name called, turning to see my nieces and sister-in-law coming out the back door to join Evie and me outside.

"How are my favorite girls?" I ask, pushing myself up to sit with my legs crisscrossed. They both practically jump into my lap, trying to hug me.

"Good!"

"Can we play?"

I don't really catch who says what to me, as they're both excited to be here.

"Sure can," I tell both of them, "and I missed you both so much." They both pull back from our group hug. I look up at both of them, bouncing my eyes between the two. "Are you sure you both haven't grown since I last saw you?" I ask in a teasing manner. I just saw them yesterday, so I know that they haven't really grown a noticeable amount overnight.

"Maybe!" Penny says, attempting to twirl in a circle.

"Careful, Pen, you don't want to hurt Evie."

"Sorry, Aunt Ry," she says, jutting her bottom lip out in the fakest pout I've ever seen.

"Hey, how are you feeling?" I ask Jillian once she joins

us outside. She sits down on one of the lounge chairs and puts her feet up. She's about six months pregnant already. I can't wait to meet my nephew in the fall. They found out just a few weeks ago that it was a boy, and Derek is over the moon excited about having a son join the family.

"Eh, feeling about as big as a house, hot all the time and I've started feeling like I've got to pee at least once an hour. I never remember it starting this early with the girls, but man, this boy is killing me."

"It will all be worth it come October."

"I know, I know. I just have to make it through the next few months," she muses.

"Well, you just sit back and relax and let me wear these girls out for you."

"You're the best, Riley."

"I know." I smirk. I love helping out, and it's not like it's a hardship to spend time with my family.

"Hey, girls!" I turn my attention back to my nieces.

"Yes?" They both give me their attention.

"What do you say we put on our swimsuits and take Evie into the pool?"

"Yes!" they both cheer out.

"We already have our suits on!" Addison tells me as she starts pulling off her shirt and shorts.

"Perfect! Then you're one step ahead of me," I tell her. I pick Evie up, holding her up like she's an airplane. I bring her in close, blowing a raspberry in the crook of her neck, making her full-on belly laugh. It's one of the best sounds ever, so I do it again, getting another squeal of laughter from her and the girls.

I lay her down and start stripping her from the outfit I'd dressed her in this morning. I thought ahead and brought out a swim diaper and one of the cute little suits that were in some of the clothes Jillian brought over now that they know they're having a boy.

"Are you ready, Aunt Ry?" Penny asks a few minutes later. While I finished getting Evie ready for the pool, Jillian made sure the girls were sun screened up. I'd put my bikini on before we came outside, so all I have to do is take off my cover up.

"I'm ready," I tell them. I grab the baby floating thing we picked up for Evie to sit in and float around the pool and help Penny and Addison get their floatation devices on. With only one adult and three kids, I feel a little better if they have them on, even though I know they can swim fairly well with all the lessons Jillian has had them in.

I count down and watch as they both jump into the water, splashing it everywhere from their cannonballs. I enter slowly, using the stairs with Evie in my arms. She shrieks with excitement when her toes first hit the water, and starts kicking her legs once they're fully submerged. She loves being in here, and we've started spending time doing just this most afternoons. It helps wear her out, and then she sleeps so well come bedtime. I've successfully gotten her on an excellent schedule, sleeping all night for about twelve straight hours. It is glorious.

I spend the next hour or so splashing around with Evie, Penelope, and Addison. The bigger girls love swimming up and playing with Evie, then getting out and jumping back into the pool. I swear they purposely try and make the biggest splash they can possibly make with their little bodies with each new jump.

"Are you ready for Daddy to be home?" I ask Addison once we're out of the pool and all drying off. We move away from the side of the pool and closer to Jillian, so she helps the girls get dried off and changed out of their suits.

"Yep! He's going to take me to lunch tomorrow!" she tells me, all excited about her plans with Derek.

"That sounds like fun. What about you, Penny?"

"I don'ts gets to go tomorrow," she pouts, and I can tell she doesn't like that.

"I'm sure Daddy will do something special with you, too," I reassure her.

"Yep, Penny's date with Daddy is the next day," Jillian says, trying to remind her daughter of that fact.

"See, Penny, Daddy wouldn't forget about you," I tell her, trying to cheer her up.

Evie starts to fuss, so we all head inside to find a snack. I sit Evie in her highchair and put a few puffs on the tray in front of her. She's just recently started eating a few things. She loves her some mashed avocado and will gnaw on practically any fruit I put in these little mesh feeder things that I found that make things safer for her to try and eat now that she's old enough to eat solid food.

"Do you mind keeping an eye on her while I go change quick?" I ask Jillian once everyone is settled in with a snack.

"Of course," she tells me, waving me off. I quickly head to my room and slip into a tank top and shorts. I was already fully dried off, so the process is quick.

"Did you want to stay for dinner?" I ask Jillian as I enter

the kitchen. The girls are just finishing the cut-up apples I gave them.

"You don't mind?"

"Of course not. I was just going to order some takeout tonight anyway."

"Then, yes. All I'd be able to muster was a drive-through on the way home, so that saves me a trip outside of the neighborhood."

"What is baby boy in the mood for?"

"Oh man, what isn't he in the mood for?" she jokes. "Some carbs sound delicious right about now, maybe pizza?"

"We can do that," I tell her, picking up my phone and placing an order for delivery. "Done. Order will be here in about forty-five minutes."

"You're a godsend and the best sister-in-law a girl could ask for."

"You're not so bad yourself," I tell her as we move out into the living room. I bring a bottle for Evie with me and prop her up in my arms as she takes hold of it. She's been able to hold it herself now for a few weeks and is insistent on doing so. The girls playing with toys keeps distracting her, so I eventually take it from her and plop her down in the jumperoo so she can play safely.

"So, anything happening between you and JJ yet?" she asks. I knew the questions were going to come again at some point.

"Nope, not that the tension between us isn't there. We've had a few close calls, that one hot-ass kiss early on. But we both try and keep our distance when it's just the two of us here and Evie isn't awake. It's for the best," I tell her, not sure who I'm trying to convince of that.

"I still don't see what the problem is. You're both consenting adults, and obviously, the attraction goes both ways. Why continue to fight it?" she asks.

"So, say we act on this attraction. What happens after that? Things would get weird, and I'm his employee. If things went bad, what would he do about Evie? It's not like he can just hire any person off the street to come to take care of her. Not many people would be willing to just move in. Not to mention, how much that would kill me to no longer be in her life, here taking care of her every day."

"But what if it's meant to be? What if you guys try it out and see where things go? Maybe he's ready to settle down. I haven't heard Derek complaining that he's going out all the time, anymore. I think that Evie has really changed him in these past few months."

"She definitely has, and you're right. He hasn't gone out partying since she arrived. He's hardly even gone out for a beer with the guys after a game. I think he might when they're on the road, since it isn't like he can come home and see her, but I don't know for sure."

"He doesn't. Nothing more than dinner with the guys," Jillian tells me. "That's what I'm saying. Derek was telling me all about how much he's changed. How much he's noticed this about JJ. How he's always talking about Evie, and much to Derek's dismay, JJ talks about you."

"Ugh. Why does life have to be so complicated?" I groan, tossing my head back on the couch.

"Welcome to adulthood." Jillian laughs next to me.

"Look at how crazy my life has been in just the last year. I divorced your brother because of his antics, and now we're *re*-married with a third kid on the way. If that doesn't say complicated, I don't know what does."

"But your situation is different. You guys have been together for a while, and it took that to wake my dumb-a-s-s," I spell the last of that word out so that the little ears don't overhear and repeat it, "brother up and realize that he was throwing away the best thing that'd ever happened to him."

"What if this," she says, spinning her finger in a circle like she's pointing out everything in this house, "is the best thing to ever happen to you? You can't tell me in one breath that me going after what I wanted, and was best for my family, was a smart move, but not do the same thing for you. My advice is to go for it, Riley. Kiss the man. Drag him to bed, strip his clothes off, and take what you want. He's not going to tell you no, and we all know that. If you're worried about your brother's reaction, don't be," she says and winks at me. "I'll distract him for you."

"He'd be pissed. Even with the changes that JJ has made these few months, Derek still tells him to stay away from me."

"Eh, he'll get over it, and if he doesn't, then I'll withhold sex from him," she says, and I see a little evil gleam shining in her eyes.

"You wouldn't!"

"Oh, I would. He'll change his tune really damn quick, or he'll just have to become friendly with his right hand again."

"I love you," I tell her just as the doorbell rings. I jump

up, going to answer the door. I hand over a tip to the delivery driver, then accept the boxes and carry them into the kitchen. "Dinner is served!" I call out to everyone and hear three sets of feet against the tile floor as they come into the kitchen.

Jillian has Evie on her hip as they all join me. I've already pulled out some paper plates and have a slice of pizza on two plates for each of the girls. I get them set up first, at the table with their pizza and two juice boxes. I've started keeping things here for them since they come over so often with me being here all the time with Evie.

"This was just what I needed," Jillian says as she finishes a second slice of pizza.

"It was," I agree with her.

"Are you going to be okay with bath and bedtime?" I ask once we're finished with dinner and I've cleaned everything up, wrapping the few leftover slices up and placing them in the fridge. "I could always follow you home and help tonight."

"I think we'll be good. They've been so helpful lately. It's like they know this baby is taking its toll on me."

"That's good. But if something changes, please call. I can always pack Evie up, and we can come over."

"Thanks, but we'll be fine. Plus, I don't want to impose on her bedtime. I know how important that is to keep babies on their schedules."

"Truer words have never been spoken," I agree.

I help Jillian get the girls packed up and out the door, then scoop Evie up and head into the bathroom to start her bath. I could tell our afternoon in the pool is catching up with her, so bedtime might be coming a little early for her tonight.

Forty minutes later and I've got a conked out Evie sleeping peacefully in her crib. I grab her laundry basket as I leave the nursery and get a load started. With a full evening by myself ahead of me, I might as well do something useful. Once JJ is home tonight, he has the following forty-eight hours off. No games, no practice, no meetings. So that means that I have at least twenty-four hours off. Not that I mind spending my time with Evie, but I'm also looking forward to a massage and pedicure. Maybe a glass of wine or, better yet, maybe Jillian and I can go out to dinner without kids. She can leave the girls with Derek, and we can have a girls' day.

I fill a glass with some lemonade, grab my Kindle from the kitchen counter, and head outside to relax in the pleasant evening air that has settled in now that the sun is going down. I get lost in my book, not even realizing how much time has passed until I hear the door slide open. I look over and see JJ standing in the doorway, looking good enough to eat.

"Hey, how was the flight home?"

"Good, uneventful, like usual," he tells me, closing the space between us and taking a seat on the chair next to me. "How was it around here?"

"Good, Jillian and the girls came over, and I took them swimming. Then we ordered pizza for dinner."

"Sounds like a good day. How was Evie?"

"Just fine. Between playing with the girls and the pool

time, she crashed a little early and hard, so I've been out here for hours just reading."

"Reading another one of your smut books?" JJ asks, a smirk tugging at the corner of his lips.

"Don't be an ass," I tell him, smacking his arm with my hand. "But if you must know, yes, it's a romance. A sports romance; baseball, to be exact," I tell him, raising an eyebrow at him.

"Hmm," is all he hums out. He runs his fingertips along the sensitive skin of my wrist that still on the armrest of his chair from me smacking his arm just a few seconds ago. My pulse races, and if the deepening smirk tells me anything, he notices. "I could show you a thing or two that you wouldn't find in the pages of one of these romances you love to read."

"You sure about that?" I ask, raising my eyebrow again at him, in challenge this time.

"Sweetheart, I could show you all kinds of things," he states. I can't tell if it's a challenge or a warning. All I know is I feel those words down to my core, and I find myself needing to rub my thighs together as I try and find some friction to relieve the ache that has settled there.

My movements do not go unnoticed. The air between the two of us crackles. Jillian's words come back to me from earlier. The encouragement to go after what I want. Is this my moment? What would JJ do if I stood up, grabbed his hand, and pulled him inside? Would he go along with it?

I don't think about it. I stand up and do just that. I grab his hand and pull him to the back door. He stops me at the threshold, turning me so that we're facing one another, standing chest to chest. I have to crank my head to look up and into his eyes when we're this close, due to our height difference. I see so many things dancing around in his eyes. Wariness, lust, and desire are just a few of the things I can pinpoint in the dark blue eyes.

I lick my lips and watch as his eyes drop to watch as my tongue slides along them. "If we cross that doorway together, I can't promise that I'll be able to stop myself from touching you, so if you don't want that to happen, you need to step back and go inside by yourself," he tells me, searching my eyes for clarity.

THIRTEEN
JUSTIN

I LOOK INTO RILEY'S EYES AND GIVE HER A FEW seconds to make a decision. I've stopped myself so many times from this exact situation playing out since she moved into my house, but that control is about to snap.

Every time I find her in those little shorts she likes to walk around in that hardly cover her ass. The bikinis she's started wearing, now that it's pool weather, drive me fucking insane. I've lost count of how many times I've had to excuse myself and go rub one out in my shower because of her being around me, consuming my every thought over the last few months.

"Last chance," I growl as my lips near hers. I slide my hands up her arms until I'm cupping her face with both of my rough hands.

"Shut up and kiss me, JJ," she whispers between us, and I do just that. My lips cover hers. Soft for the first second or two. Then she opens for me, and I take it all. I'm a greedy bastard. One that hasn't been laid in months. And my dick is all over the fact that I've got a beautiful woman in my arms and pressed up against my body.

I drop my hands to her waist and then to her ass. I cup those perfect cheeks in my palms and give them a good squeeze before I lift her up. Her legs go around my waist as she locks her feet together, securing her around me. My cock is hard as a steel beam, and her center pressed against me just above it is driving me fucking crazy. I spin us until I can push her back against the wall next to the door. I grind against her, all while still devouring her mouth.

Riley tugs at my shirt, and I break the kiss long enough to pull it off over my head. I tug at her tank top, and it joins my T-shirt on the floor a second later. I drag my fingertip along the top of her lacy bra then follow the path with my lips. I drop my mouth a little lower, flicking my tongue over her nipples, and revel in the fact that they pebble as I do just that. The moans that fall from her lips have me almost coming in my pants like I'm a fourteen-year-old boy seeing his first set of tits.

"You like that, baby?" I ask against her skin.

"Yes!" she moans, and I reach behind her, finding the clasp of her bra, and flick it open one-handed. It joins our shirts on the floor moments later, and I return to sucking on her nipples. They're perfect. The prettiest dusty rose color, darkening as I suck and roll them between my fingertips.

I kiss my way back up her chest, finding a few sweet spots along her neck and jaw that have her purring like a cat. I devour her mouth once again when I reach it.

I've had enough of making out against the wall like a teenager, so I step back and carefully make my way through the house, stopping only once we're inside my room. I close the door, then pin Riley against it.

"I need to taste you," I tell her as I set her down on her feet, then drop to my knees. I look up at her as I tug her shorts off her hips. She steps out of them, one foot at a time, our eye contact never breaking. Once the shorts are on the floor a few feet away from us where they landed after I tossed them, I take my fill of her almost naked body. I feel her creamy smooth skin as I run my fingertips from her ankle up the backs of her calves, over her knees, and up the backs of her thighs. I bring my hands around to the front, running the pads of my thumbs over her clit that is still covered by a scrap of lace. It is sexy as fuck, so I lean forward and kiss it. I suck in a deep breath, filling my lungs with her scent. I can smell her arousal, and it makes my cock harden even more in my pants.

I watch her for any signs that she doesn't want this. Her chest heaves as she sucks in a few breaths, waiting for my next move. I spread her legs a little farther apart, making room for my shoulders. Once I fit between her thighs, I move her thong to the side and then run my tongue from her core to her clit, and I swear she levitates off the ground. I pull back slightly and look up at her, and the blissed-out look on her face tells me this is precisely what she wanted. I return to my previous position, alternating between sucking and flicking her clit with my tongue, and slipping it into her pussy as it clenches. I move back up to suck on her clit, just as I slide a finger inside her. She's so fucking tight, and it's at that moment I recall what she told Jillian a few months ago. She's so tight because she's a fucking virgin.

"You like that, baby?" I say against her clit. My finger slides in and out of her pussy as I fuck her slowly with it.

"Yes," she pants. "Please don't stop. I'm so close."

"That's it, baby. Come on my tongue," I tell her as I replace my finger with my tongue. I fuck her, my tongue slipping inside her as she grinds her pussy against my face, riding out her orgasm. I lap at every drop of her sweetness as she comes. I'm going to become addicted to the taste of her, I can tell already. I stroke her through her release, waiting patiently as she comes down from the high that hits your body after an intense orgasm. I look up at her, watching her until she looks down at me. The smile that fills her face has me ready to slide my cock inside her and take her until I fill her with every drop of cum that is built up in my body.

"I never imagined you on your knees for me," she says into the silence.

"I'll gladly get on my knees for you anytime. You've got the sweetest pussy," I tell her, then swipe my tongue along her slit once again. "And I don't get on my knees, but for you, I'll do it anytime, anyplace."

"You can't be serious," she stammers out. I stand up, my knees popping from being down so long. I pick her back up, wrapping her legs around my waist.

"I'm as serious as a heart attack," I tell her as I take her mouth with my own. I let her taste her own release. "I was never about dropping to my knees for anyone else. That was always the place for the woman to be, but I see the errors of my past." I smirk at her.

"You're such an ass," she says, smacking my chest.

"Former ass. I'm a changed man now."

"Mhmm," she hums. "Think you can take me over to that big bed of yours?" she asks, pointing over my shoulder at my king size bed.

"Is that what you what? I don't know if I can stop myself from fucking you if you touch my bed."

"I'm sure," she says, a little nervousness coming through her voice, but also a whole lot of confidence. Confidence that I find sexy as fuck.

I close the distance between my door and bed, sitting Riley down on the mattress and boxing her in on the bed. "Tell me what you want," I tell her, my voice as gravely as it gets. I want this woman more than I've ever wanted anyone in my life.

"I want you to slide that big cock of yours inside me and fuck me until I can't walk tomorrow." My eyes about pop out of my sockets at her boldness.

"I don't want to hurt you," I warn her, my eyes dropping to her pussy. The one that hardly could take *one* of my fingers. How in the hell is she going to handle my cock? The cock that's at least the diameter of three, if not four, of my fingers. She's going to be so tight I might not make it more than one pump before I'm going off.

"You won't." She smirks.

"Are you sure?" I ask her one last time. I don't think she knows that I know she's still a virgin, and I don't want to make this awkward for her. I stand to my full height and drop my pants and boxers. I palm my cock, giving it a few good strokes. I watch as Riley's eyes widen just a little as she takes in my size. She licks her lips as if she's ready to lick a lollipop, and I feel that all the way to my balls. "Want a taste?" I cockily ask.

"Yes," she says, grinning up at me. She scoots to the edge of the mattress, her legs between mine. I widen my stance. I hold still as she tentatively reaches out and wraps her fist around my shaft. Her skin touching mine for the first time is like a brand. My skin is sizzling everywhere she touches. I let her stroke me a few times before I wrap my fist around hers, showing her just how I like it.

She leans forward once again, this time she flicks her tongue out and across the head of my cock. She takes the bead of pre-cum off my tip and moans before sucking it into her mouth like a goddamn lollipop. I don't know how long I can last with her sucking my cock like this, but I grit my teeth and let her have her fun. When she finally breaks off from my cock, I reach over to the nightstand and pull out a condom. I tear the packet open with my teeth, pulling out the latex and rolling it down my shaft.

I slip my fingers into the waist of her thong and tug it off. I grab the bottle of lube from the drawer, as well, coating two of my fingers in it so I can ease them inside of her pussy. The first one slips in, her muscles clenching around it. I give her a few slow thrusts before I add in the second finger. Her breath hitches slightly, but her body relaxes as I start to move the two fingers inside.

"You ready for my cock?" I ask as I work her up with my fingers. I think if I have her nice and loose and ready to come, that it will ease the pain of my cock stretching her.

She nods her head yes, but that isn't enough for me. I

need her words. "Words, Riley," I tell her, dropping a chaste kiss to her lips.

"Fuck me, Justin."

I growl at her use of my full name. I strum her clit, working her up and close to another orgasm. Just as I feel her core start to flutter around my fingers, I pull them from her pussy, bringing them to my mouth to lick clean. I add a few drops of the lube to the head of my cock, running it around the latex quickly before I line my tip up with her entrance. I lock my eyes with Riley, hold my cock with one hand, and continue strumming her clit with the other as I push in.

Her face pinches as my head slips in, and I still. "You sure you're ready?" I ask, not wanting to push her into something she's not ready for.

"We're not stopping now." she tells me, and I feel the heels of her feet dig into my ass as she attempts to push me in further. I pull out, then line up again and slip back in, this time going a little further. Pull out, press back in. I do this repeatedly, until I finally thrust all the way in, and her cries still me immediately.

"Fuck!" I grit out, but as I go to pull out, she stops me in my tracks.

"Don't, please don't pull out." So, I don't. I stay as still as I can, and soon her muscles start to relax around my cock. I begin to move slightly, only pulling out a little bit then snapping my hips back. My movements are met by moans that I'm realizing are pleasure-filled and not pain.

"You doing okay?" I ask a few thrusts later.

"Perfect," she tells me, a smile on her lips. I take that

look as my opening to change things up slightly, so I speed up my thrusts just a little bit. I slide my cock almost all the way out of her pussy, only leaving the tip in, before I snap my hips back. My balls hit her ass, and her cries fill my ears. I roll my hips, grinding my pelvis against her clit with each thrust. When my pelvis isn't grinding against it, I rub it with the pad of my thumb. I can feel her building up for a release, so I drop down and capture her mouth with my own. I fuck her pussy and mouth with identical thrusts, swallowing her cries as she finally crests over the edge. Her orgasm triggers my own, and I snap my hips one last time, emptying myself into the condom.

I break the kiss and suck in air as my head drops to the bed just above her shoulder. I slip my cock from her pussy, a small smear of blood on the condom, and I hope like hell she doesn't regret this in the morning. I kiss her one more time before I go into the bathroom and dispose of the condom. I grab a washcloth and run it under the faucet until it's warm. I ring it out before taking it to her. I'd clean her up, but that seems a little personal, and I'm not quite sure where we stand. I know I just fucked her, hell, took her virginity, but I don't want her uncomfortable. Hell, I don't want her leaving my bed, at this point.

"Thank you," she says, taking the washcloth from me and pulling me from my thoughts.

"You're welcome," I tell her and give her a minute to clean up. "I didn't hurt you, did I?" I ask once she's done.

"It was a little painful, at first, but the pain subsided after a minute."

I sit back down on the bed, pulling her with me as I lay

down. She settles in, her head on my chest as her fingers trace shapes on my skin. My arm goes around her, settling my hand on her hip. "It was your first time?" I state, wanting to get it out there. Let her know, I know.

I feel her go rigid in my arms; her fingers stop moving along my abs. "Riley, look at me," I tell her quietly as I tip her face up so we can look at each other.

"How'd you know?" she asks, then closes her eyes tightly.

"Besides the fact that your pussy was tighter than a vise grip? I might have heard you tell Jillian a few months ago." Her eyes fly open, and she looks at me with huge eyes. I can't tell if she's pissed or embarrassed.

"Yeah, it's not like I was waiting for any specific reason," she tells me, and I remember her saying the same thing to Jillian.

"So why me? Why tonight?" I ask, curious as to the answer to that.

"Why not you? Why not tonight?" she throws back to me.

"Your first time should be special," I tell her, bringing my free hand up to skim over the delicate skin of her nose and cheeks. She's got a few freckles dotting her perfect skin, and I, all of a sudden, want to search her entire body for more and trace them with my tongue. "You're beautiful, you know that?" I drop my lips to hers, an incredible need to kiss her, in this exact moment, washing over my body. She relaxes into the kiss. One that starts out easy, lazy almost. One that you'd think was between lifelong lovers.

"It was perfect," she says against my lips when we break

the kiss. "I couldn't have planned a better first time if I tried." She sucks in a breath. "But please promise me that this won't make things weird between us. I can't stop working for you. I love your daughter like she's my own, and it would kill me to no longer be here with her all the time."

"Riley," I say her name, trying to get her to stop rambling. "Riley, you're not going anywhere," I tell her, but I don't think she hears me, so I kiss her again. It's the only way I can think to get her to stop talking. I roll us so that she's pinned beneath me, which wasn't the smartest move on my part, as my cock is now hard again now that it's nestled between her legs, but it did what I needed it to do, and that got her attention. "Riley, you're not going anywhere if I have anything to say about it. I need you, Evie needs you. We'd be lost without *you*. She's priority number one. We'll figure out what this is between us. But I can tell you that I don't want it to be a one-time thing. Now that I've had you, I know I'm going to want you again and again."

"What about Derek?" she asks, her voice hardly above a whisper.

"He'll deal," I tell her, not really caring what Derek thinks about us together. Would he kick my ass if he knew I took his sister's virginity tonight? He absolutely would, but what he doesn't know won't kill him. I'll eventually have to have a little chat with him if things move forward, but that can wait until we're there. "Let me deal with him when the time is right. He doesn't need to be privy to our personal business," I assure her.

"Okay," she agrees, a little easier than I expected.

FOURTEEN
RILEY

THE PAST WEEK HAS BEEN A WHIRLWIND OF A WEEK. I thought my first week here with JJ was crazy, but this one might just top that one. It's been a blur of stolen kisses during the day and delicious nights spent between the sheets as we lose ourselves in each other's bodies.

I gather Evie's things, placing her in the stroller so that we can walk over to my brother's house. The guys are gone at practice, and we've been cooped up inside the past two days, thanks to the rain, so getting outside is a must today.

I take my time pushing the stroller over to Derek and Jillian's, taking what I like to think of as the long way around. It gives me a good solid two miles winding through the neighborhood, and I can use every one of those steps today. My body has never felt this deliciously sore before, but I love every moment of it. Justin is an expert when it comes to making my body feel on fire. His touch is like a brand against my skin.

"Hey!" Jillian calls out when I walk through the door. I left the stroller in the garage and have Miss Evie on my hip.

"How's it going around here?" I ask her as I set the diaper bag down on one of the bar stools. I hand Evie over to Jillian, who smothers her cheeks in kisses. The girl has the best cheeks to nom on. It's really too bad that we have to keep her out of the spotlight, as she could seriously be the next Gerber or Carters baby, she's that stinking cute.

"It's going. I was just about to get some lunch going for the girls. Are you hungry?" Jillian asks, setting Evie into the highchair they keep out since we're over here so often.

"Absolutely. Need help?" I offer.

"I was just making some sandwiches and cutting up some fruit. Simple is my game plan this week."

"Sounds perfect. I can get the fruit cut up," I offer. I pull out the puffs from the diaper bag and place some in front of Evie, along with a sippy cup that I've introduced to her this week. She still isn't sure about it, and I end up picking it up off the floor a hundred or so times, as she thinks it's hilarious to drop it over and over again. Once she's got a few things to keep her occupied, I pull the fruit from the fridge and get it washed before I start cutting it up for everyone.

"So, spill," Jillian says a few minutes later.

"Spill what?" I ask, trying to act as innocent as possible.

"Something's different, I can tell. I just can't put my finger on it."

"I don't know what you're talking about," I say, but can feel the smile trying to pull at the corners of my lips as a blush heats my cheeks.

"You're such a liar!" Jillian says, pointing her finger in my direction. "Did something *finally* happen between you and JJ?" she questions, and I can feel the heat radiating from my cheeks.

"Shhh," I shush her then look around for the girls. I absolutely do not want them to overhear any of this and possibly repeat it around Derek. That's all we need. "Yes..." I say, stalling. That smile that was threatening to fill my lips is now filling my face as I think back on the last week. "We're together?" I tell her, but it comes out more like a question. "We're seeing where things go, but you can't say *anything*! We want to keep it just between the two of us until we know what this is."

"I knew it!" Jillian says, punching her fists into the air like she's won a prize. "So, does this mean that you've no longer got your V-card?"

"Correct," I tell her, looking up to catch her reaction to my confession.

"I'm going to assume from the look on your face that it has been a good week, then?" she says, a knowing smirk tugging at her lips.

"Yeah," I say, once again thinking about just this morning and the *dirty, dirty* things JJ did to me in the shower before Evie woke up. "Things have been *very, very* good. He's a very experienced partner and knows how to use what he's got, expertly," I tell her, another blush heating my cheeks.

"Get it, girl. Just make sure he treats you right."

"Don't worry, he's treating me just fine," I tell her as I finish cutting up the fruit. She's plated sandwiches for all of us, so I add a scoop of fruit to the girls' plates for her as she sets them out on the table. I grab a couple of juice boxes from the fridge as Jillian calls them to the dining room to eat.

"Aunt RyRy!" Penelope calls out when she sees me. "When's you get here?" she asks as I bend down to pick her up in a bear hug.

"Just a few minutes ago. Evie and I came to hang out for the afternoon, how's that sound?"

"Yea!" she exclaims as I put her down. Addison gives me a side hug as she passes by, beelining it to the table. She must be starving to blow past me like that.

Jillian and I join the girls at the table with our own plates, but change the conversation now that we've got little ears that can pick up on things.

"What should we do after lunch?" I ask Penny and Addy.

"The park!" Addy calls out.

"The zoo!" Penny suggests next.

"Both of those sound fun!" I tell them. "I don't know, what do you think, Mommy?" I ask, directing my question to Jillian.

"We could maybe go up to the zoo for a little while, but in order to do that, we have to have an hour of quiet time after lunch."

"But, Mommy, I's not tired!" Penny tries to complain.

"Sorry, P, if you want to go check on the animals, those are the rules. Plus, baby Evie will need her nap before we can go."

"Fine," she pouts.

"How about this," Jillian says to her, gathering her attention. "How about I put on a movie, quietly, and you lay down on the couch. You don't have to fall asleep if you're not tired, but you do have to stay quiet and watch the movie."

"Okay, Momma," she agrees right away to Jillian's compromise.

"Does that work for you?" Jillian confirms with me.

"Sure does. Evie and I didn't really have any firm plans other than hanging out here with you guys for the next few hours. I'll just need to pop over to the house to grab her car seat."

"LOOK AT THE GIRAFFES!" I EXCLAIM TO THE GIRLS. WE watch as they come to the railing where patrons can feed them lettuce that they purchase from a little booth next to the enclosure. Jillian is in line buying a bundle for all of us to feed to them. I swear this is their favorite part of the zoo.

"Aww, look, RyRy, it's a baby one!" Addison tells me, pointing out one of the baby giraffes.

"Aww, she sure is cute," I tell her as we get a little closer to the railing. I park the stroller right up next to it so that Evie can see through it to the animals. She must see some of the animals as she starts to get excited in her seat. One of the giraffes must notice her and think that she's got a snack for him as he sticks his head through the railings and flicks his tongue out at her. I can't help but laugh at the face she makes when the giraffe's tongue licks her face. I quickly grab my phone from my back pocket and snap a picture as it does it again.

"Auntie, it's licking her!" Penny shrieks in excitement.

"I know!" I laugh right along with her. Evie still doesn't know what to think about this, and starts to fuss. I move the stroller back a bit so that the animals can no longer reach her. I grab a wipe from the bag and wipe her face off where he kissed her.

"I watched it all unfold from the line," Jillian says as she reaches my side. "It was pretty funny to watch it go down," she tells me as she hands her girls each a few pieces of lettuce.

"It sure was, and I got a few pictures," I tell her, handing over my phone so she can look at them. She swipes right, flipping through the pictures until her eyebrows fly up.

"Well, now this is an interesting picture," she says, flashing me a shit-eating grin. *Fuck, I forgot about that.* JJ grabbed my phone this morning and snapped a picture of the two of us curled up together in bed. Thank god we've got the sheet pulled up, as we were both naked when it was taken. That was before our shower escapades, but after the first set of orgasms he brought us to this morning. "Y'all look good together, just like I knew you would."

"Yeah," I sigh. "It's been a whirlwind week, for sure," I tell her. I'm sure I've got a dreamy look on my face. It still feels like one big dream.

"Just be careful and use protection. Do I need to have the birth control talk with you?" she asks. I look around at the other people in close proximity to us and feel my cheeks heat up.

"Jill!" I practically squeal. "Could you say it any louder?" I ask, feeling embarrassed.

"Sorry," she says as she looks around. "That came out a little louder than I planned it to."

"To answer your question, we're careful. Protection every time and no, *Mom,* I don't need the BC talk. I've been on it for a while to help regulate my cycles."

"Okay. As long as you're safe, that's all that I care about. Two under two is hard, trust me," she says, flashing me a smile before looking down at the girls. They've fed the giraffes all of the lettuce that she bought, so we start herding them toward the next animal enclosure.

"I'm home!" JJ calls out as the door from the garage closes.

"In the kitchen," I call out to him.

"How are my girls today?" he asks, stopping to kiss the top of Evie's head before he stops behind me. He slides my hair off my shoulder, exposing the side of my neck. He drops his lips just below my ear, sucking lightly, which drives me fucking insane. His hands rest on my hips as he holds me still against him. I can feel his hard ridges against my back as he presses against me.

"We're good," I say a little breathlessly all of a sudden. "Went to the zoo for a little while this afternoon with Jillian and the girls. I got some cute pictures of Evie! I'll Airdrop them to you in a few minutes," I tell him as I finish prepping the chicken to go on the grill for dinner.

"Sounds like a good day," he replies.

"It was. How was your day?"

"Practice like normal. Derek was on my ass about why I've been so happy lately. I think he's getting suspicious."

That stops me in my tracks. The last thing that I want to happen is for my brother and Justin's friendship to be affected by our relationship.

"Justin," I sigh his name. "We've got to either stop this or tell him."

"We're not fucking stopping this, I'll tell him. Just give me a little bit. Okay?" he says, grabbing my hands in his after I've washed and dried them off.

"Okay, but make it soon. I hate feeling like I'm sneaking around. Plus, Jillian knows now. She promised me she wouldn't say anything, but she guessed, and then I couldn't deny it if I tried. And then, on top of all that, she saw that picture you snapped of us this morning," I tell him.

Justin pulls me until my front is flush with his. He's leaning against the counter, which helps some with our height difference. "That was a pretty epic picture. I could still taste you on my lips," he says as he brings his lips to mine in the softest kiss I've ever experienced. "You were still blissfully relaxed from the orgasm I'd just given you with my tongue," he says as he drops kisses along my jawline. "And another one with my cock." He sucks my earlobe between his teeth, scraping them along the sensitive skin.

I melt into him, loving the way he can wake my body up in a matter of seconds. Between the way he touches me and his dirty words, I'm wet and ready for him to take me to bed.

"Bawwww, yaaaa," Evie babbles, pulling our attention from each other and to her. She's in her jumperoo that I pulled into the kitchen for her to play in while I prepped dinner.

We both watch as she entertains herself between bouncing and all the connected toys on that thing.

"Think you can go get the grill fired up?" I ask him, stepping out from between his legs.

"Sure can," he says as he takes his ball cap off his head, flipping it backward. I don't know what it is about him in that hat that makes my knees go weak, but damn does he look hot in it, especially when he turns it backwards.

"Don't hurt yourself staring at me like that," he says, swiping a thumb across my bottom lip. I almost flick my tongue out as the pad of his thumb slides across it, but hold back. We need to get dinner made, and then he needs to spend time with his daughter before it's time for her to go to bed. Then, and only then, can we do whatever it is that we want to do to one another.

"I wasn't staring," I insist.

"Mhmm," he hums. "And I wasn't balls deep inside you *twice* this morning, making you scream my name."

He gives me a smoldering look as he grabs the platter of chicken and the vegetable basket to place on the grill once it is warmed up and ready. "What, no comeback?" he asks once he's out of my reach.

I hold up my hand, waving it as if I'm telling him to go away. "No need to get all cocky," I call out at him once he's outside.

"Last I checked, you liked my cock."

"Justin!" I whirl around, facing the door, my eyes bulging out a little bit. "Little ears, remember?" I ask him, looking down at Evie.

"It isn't like she can repeat me yet," he says, giving me a slightly sheepish grin. "Can you, baby girl?" he says, his voice morphing into the cutest damn baby-ish voice I've ever heard come from a grown-ass man as he talks to his daughter.

"She might not be able to now, but it is coming sooner than you think, and it's going to bite you in the ass one of these days."

"I guess I'll have to cross that bridge when we get there," he says, then turns his attention back to the grill. I finish up with the pasta salad I was putting together, taking it out to the table on the patio. I set the table, getting everything out just as he pulls the veggies and chicken off the grill. I bring Evie outside and place her in the highchair, setting a few things on the tray for her to pick at. JJ and I both dig in to the food we've made until our bellies are full.

Justin takes Evie from her highchair once we're finished with dinner. He plays with her for a little bit before it's time for her bath and bedtime. I take care of the dishes while he spends time with her then retreat back outside with a small glass of wine. When he's home in the evenings, this has become our regular routine. He wants to spend as much time as he can with her, and I think that it's essential that he has some time with just the two of them.

I hear some shuffling in the house, so head inside to see what he might be up to. "Hey, babe?" he calls out from down the hall, just as I round the corner and run right into my brother's chest. *Fuck.*

"Babe?" Derek barks out.

"Oh, shit," I hear Justin swear as he comes out of his room and finds Derek and I standing toe to toe.

"Justin, why the fuck are you calling my *sister* babe?" Derek asks, then sucks in a deep breath as he looks up at the ceiling.

"Derek, please." I say his name, my voice steady, but I can hear the wariness in it, so I know that he can, as well.

He whirls around, facing off with JJ. "Talk. Now. Johnson," Derek barks out, calling Justin by his last name.

Derek tracks Justin's movements as he comes to stand next to me. He pulls me into his side, his arm coming around me as he rests his hand on my hip. It's possessive. It's a statement without words. One that my brother doesn't like one bit, if the look on his face tells me anything.

"What do you want to know?" JJ finally breaks the silence between the three of us.

"I want to know why the fuck you've got your hands on my sister. Why you're calling her *babe.* I could have sworn that I've told you to keep your fucking hands to yourself and that she was off-limits," he growls. He's getting madder as each word passes his lips.

"Why don't you calm down," I interject, not wanting Derek to lose his cool.

"Calm down. Really, Riley?" he scoffs at me.

"That's enough," Justin barks. "We're together, seeing where things go. We fought it but decided, as two consenting adults, that we wanted to see where this went.

We didn't want to hurt you or keep it from you forever, but we also didn't feel like you needed to know right away. We wanted to make sure that it was more than just two people being around each other all the time, scratching an itch," Justin tells him.

Derek's eyes bounce between the two of us. I can see the war raging in him. He wants to be pissed off, but I can also tell that he wants me and Justin to be happy, even if that means that we're happy *together*.

"And how long has this been going on?" he asks.

"About a week," I tell him. "But honestly, we've been dancing around it since right after I moved in," I tell him. We might as well be honest with him, without spelling out every single detail about our relationship.

"I knew something was up with you this week," he says, shaking his head. "Never did I think it was you fucking my sister."

"It isn't like that, man," JJ states, "I care about Riley. I'm not out there chasing every woman who looks my way anymore. I see the value in what this could be, and I don't intend to fuck it up."

"You better not," Derek tells him. "If you hurt her, I'd have to hurt you, and I don't want to have to do that."

"I'm not saying I won't mess up, you know better than anyone that sometimes we do stupid shit, but I don't intend to ever hurt her on purpose. She's too important to Evie, to me," JJ says, looking down at me. I can see the sincerity in his eyes. I can read between the lines of what he isn't saying. Not that I'd expect any declarations this early on, but with the friendship we've built over the last few months, the trust that he has in me to basically raise his daughter as a stand-in mother, takes a lot of trust and love, on some level. "So, you can either get on board with us being together and support us, or the door is over there, don't let it hit you on the way out. I'm not going to stop this just because you don't like it."

I'm a little shocked that JJ was so straightforward with Derek. We'd never explicitly talked about what he'd say when he finally told Derek about us, but we also didn't expect Derek to walk in on us. Thank god he didn't walk in while we were making out or having sex. That would have been embarrassing and he would have been so pissed. I can only imagine what Derek would have done if that had happened.

Derek grunts out. I'm not sure if it's an approval? Or maybe just him conceding to JJ's statement.

"Now that we've got that out of the way, what did you need from us tonight, big brother?" I ask Derek as sweetly as I can.

"Was just coming over to have a beer."

"Well, don't let me stand in your way," I tell the guys as I step back. JJ grabs two beers from the fridge, and I watch as they both head outside to the patio. I decide to give them this time to grunt it out between the two of them. I grab my Kindle and curl up on the couch, quickly getting lost betweyen the pages of the book I've been sucked into.

FIFTEEN
JUSTIN

"You're sure you are okay with this?" I ask Riley again. "I know it messes with Evie's nap schedule."

"Of course, I'm fine with it. We wouldn't miss the family day for anything," she says, bouncing Evie on her lap. Riley has dressed my baby girl in my jersey, well, a tiny version that has 'Daddy's Girl' where my last name goes. It was a present from the front office, one that they give all players when they have a baby.

We've been successful in keeping Evie out of the spotlight, for the most part. Having my PR company send out a press release just as my attorney filed paperwork with the courts worked well. I ended up answering some questions a few days after that, but since then, the press has left me alone when it comes to my daughter, and for that, I'm grateful.

"I have a surprise for you," Riley says as she pulls her bottom lip in between her teeth. She's come out of her shell so much since moving in here, but I can always tell when she's nervous about something, as she bites her bottom lip.

"Do you now?" I ask, quirking a brow up in question.

"Close your eyes," she says, and I can feel her stand up off the couch. She places Evie on my lap, and I put my hands on her torso to hold her still. "Okay, you can open them," she says. I do just that, looking first at my daughter, and not seeing anything different, then I look up at Riley. She's standing with her back to me and is looking over her shoulder, a nervous smile tugging at the edges of her lips. I take in her back, and the vision in front of me has my dick hardening. Riley has my jersey on. One that fits her like a fucking glove. Seeing my name and number across her back has me thinking all kinds of crazy things. Long-term, permanent, put a ring on it, have more of my babies, kind of thoughts.

"Fuck," I murmur under my breath.

"You like?" she says, biting that lip once again.

"I more than like," I tell her, holding my hand out for her to grab. I move Evie to my left leg and pull Riley onto my right. "Seeing you with this jersey on makes me want to do very naughty and dirty things to you," I tell her as I nuzzle my nose along her neck, following it with sucking kisses. I can feel the goose bumps as they break out on her skin at my perusal. "You just wait until tonight. I'll be fucking you while you wear nothing but this jersey." I suck her earlobe between my lips, nipping at it before I slide my tongue over it to calm the sting left from my teeth.

"Mhmm..." she hums. "If I'd have known wearing your

jersey would have gotten this kind of welcoming response, I would have done it a long time ago."

"Is that so? And how would you have played off having my number on your back and not your brother's?"

She shrugs her shoulders at me then gives me better access to her neck. This isn't the most natural position to be making out in, nor is it the best time, seeing how I have my daughter in one hand. Thank fuck she's usually a pretty calm and chill baby and goes with the flow most of the time. "When do you have to go?" she asks, pulling away from my wandering lips.

"Soon," I tell her, running a hand through my hair. "What time do you plan to head to the ballpark?"

"Jillian is going to swing by around twelve thirty. I'll plan to feed little miss, here, around noon, that way she's got lunch before we go. Then maybe she'll get a little nap in during the drive over. I plan to pack the carrier so that I can hold her hands-free, if needed."

"Okay, and come down by the dugout. Security will know to let you pass, and then you can come out onto the field."

"Got it! I'll have Jillian by my side, and I know she's a pro at this, so I plan to just follow her."

"Are you going to let them include you in the pictures?" I ask, curious as to her answer. We talked about making our relationship public now that it is out in the open amongst our family.

"I guess so," she says, that nervous tell coming back. I reach up, cupping her cheek as I slide my thumb along her bottom lip, pulling it from her teeth. I lean in, bringing my lips to hers. I gently suck her bottom lip, razing it with my own teeth.

"Needed my own taste." I smile against her lips. "You're worrying this lip down to nothing."

"I don't even realize when I'm doing it."

"I know. That's why I stopped you." I flash her a wink.

Evie starts to squirm in my arms. She must be tired of not being the center of attention right now.

"Come here, baby girl. Daddy has to go to work," Riley says to her as if she can understand everything that is going on.

She stands up, Evie in her arms now. I sit back and take in my girls standing in front of me. Evie looks so comfortable and perfect in Riley's arms. I can tell she's relaxed as she rests her head against Riley's shoulder, burrowing her little face into Riley's neck, almost the same way that I do it.

"If you don't get moving, you're going to be late," Riley reminds me.

"I know," I tell her, still looking at her and Evie. "Just enjoying the view of my girls together. Both of you with my jersey on. It's going to be an exciting time, I'll have both of you in the stands cheering for me, not that Evie will remember it."

"She might not, but I'm sure you will," she tells me sweetly.

"Yeah," I say as she slides a hand along my cheek. I turn my face and kiss the center of her palm before I stand up and then drop a kiss to my daughter's head. "Love you, baby girl, see you later," I tell her before I give Riley one last chaste kiss. "I'll see you later, as well," I say as I smack her ass.

"Watch it, mister," she calls out as a laugh escapes her lips. I know she isn't mad one bit about the slap to her ass. If I'm not mistaken, she was *asking* for me to spank her last night when I was buried balls deep inside of her.

I shake all memories of the two of us naked together from the forefront of my mind and head for the field.

"STAND HERE AND LOOK THAT WAY," AN OLDER WOMAN calls out, pointing at a camera set up a few feet away. "Adults, keep looking at the camera, we'll do our best to get your child's attention and looking at the camera," she says as they fidget with getting Riley and I situated just how they want us for the family day picture. I was elated when Riley told me she'd participate today, not as Derek's sister or Evie's nanny, but as my girlfriend. It is still strange to refer to her like that. I feel a little old to be using a word that feels so childish, but alas, that is what she is. My girlfriend, and Evie's live-in nanny.

"Great job!" the woman calls out a few moments later. They must have gotten the shots they needed right away as they let up and call over the next family that is ready for their picture.

"Justin!" another voice calls out, this time from someone within the press group that was invited to be down on the field with the players and their family members before the game. "Can we get a picture of you with your family?" the young reporter calls out. I vaguely recognize her from one of the online sports blogs. They tend to toe the line between trash and real. They love to really twist things around from the way they really happen, so I'm not super interested in giving her much, but a picture we can do, I guess. It isn't like there aren't going to be a thousand cell phone pictures floating around of me with Evie and Riley by the end of the game.

"Sure, a quick picture is fine," I tell her as I shift Evie up higher in my arms. I drape my free arm around Riley's shoulders and pull her into my side. She rests her hand against my chest, and I look down just as she looks up at me. I realize that we've got matching goofy smiles on our faces.

"Keep it clean," Derek mumbles from a few feet away from us, and I can't help but laugh at his grumbling.

"Of course," I lobby back at him. "There are small children here, after all. Wouldn't want to scar them," I tell him, giving him shit just because I know I'm under his skin, and he's still a little pissed about the whole dating his sister thing. After our beer on the patio a week ago, when he found out about us, things have been okay between the two of us. He didn't punch me in the face, which, if I'm honest, I really expected him to do.

"Who's with you?" the reporter calls out, bringing my attention back her way. Riley stiffens slightly in my arm, so I drop my eyes to hers.

"We still good?" I say, only loud enough for Riley and Evie to hear me. She nods her head slightly, never breaking eye contact with me. Knowing she's still on board with us coming out, I look back up at the reporter. "This is my girlfriend, Riley, and this is my daughter, Evie," I tell her. It feels weird to be introducing them to everyone, but it's probably time I did so.

"How long have you been off the market? How old is the baby? Have you finalized the custody case?" the reporter calls out question after question, not allowing me to answer anything.

"Thank you for the questions, but our players are going to have a few minutes with their family before getting ready for the game. They'll be available again after the game for further game-related questions," Carmen, one of the team's PR people, responds for me.

She stepped in at the exact perfect time, effectively cutting off all the reporter's prying questions. Even without quotes from me answering them, I'm sure she'll weave up a story to post by the time the game is over tonight.

"Where are you sitting?" I ask Riley as we step away from the crowd.

"The family section. My tickets are right with Jillian and the girls' seats."

"Okay, I'll be looking for you," I tell her, dropping a quick peck against her cheek.

"Keep your eyes on the ball, we don't need any bad plays," she teases.

"My eyes are always on the ball." I smirk at her. "On a serious note, be careful who sits around you. I wouldn't put it past that chick reporter to somehow get a seat close to the family section so she can eavesdrop on everyone, trying to find out anything she can weave into one of her stories."

"I'll be as diligent as I can be," she assures me. I know

she wouldn't purposely talk or give out information, but it still worries me now that we've gone public with this. They're going to be trying to dig up anything they can on her, and it won't be long before they figure out that she's Derek's sister and Evie's nanny. "Now, get out there and win us a ball game. Little miss, here, needs to have a win for her first game watching her daddy kick butt." She takes Evie from my arms and places her in the carrier she's got strapped around her waist.

I smile once again at my girls before giving them each one last kiss. A quick slap to Riley's ass, and they're off to their seats while I go get my head ready for the game.

"The Curve Ball, We Never Saw Coming!"

I REREAD THE HEADLINE, ROLLING MY EYES SO DAMN hard that I'm a little surprised they don't roll right out of my damn head.

Has the most eligible bachelor on the Indianapolis Lightning roster changed his ways and settled down? Who was the mysterious woman at his side at yesterday's family day? Justin "JJ" Johnson told reporters that the woman joining him for the team's family day was his girlfriend. Little has been found on the mysterious woman. He only referred to her by her first name, Riley. We're dedicated to bringing you up to speed on this developing story as more

information is confirmed to us by our sources.
Johnson also had his infant daughter with him, one of
the rare public events he's allowed her to attend
since the news broke that she was born. He was
awarded full custody of the child last month after his
petition to the courts went unchallenged by the
minor's biological mother, who doesn't appear to be
in the picture. During the game, his daughter was
attended to by his girlfriend. She watched the game
from the friends and family section, sitting beside
starting pitcher Derek Smyth's wife, Jillian Smyth,
and their two daughters.

I close out of the article, not needing to read any more of this "reporter's" crap article. I knew she was just there to try and drum up non-existent drama or to dig in to my personal life. I get along with most of the press that follows the team around, but the ones like her, that are just there to try and find the dirt on anyone, rub me so wrong. She's no better than the paparazzi that take pictures when we're out grocery shopping or trying to have a meal out with friends or family.

"Morning!" Riley says cheerily as she walks into the kitchen. My dick hardens as I take in her sweaty appearance. The way her tank top clings to her skin has me itching to remove it with my teeth; sweat be damned.

"How was your run?" I ask, doing my best to keep my voice level.

"Really good," she says, taking a large drink of her water bottle. "Kept a nine thirty pace for all five miles."

"That's great, babe."

"I'm going to go take a quick shower," she says, setting her bottle down on the counter.

"Want some company?" I call after her.

Laughing at me, she calls back, "Someone's got to look after Evie. Maybe next time."

At the mention of my daughter, I look over and watch as she pulls one of the toys attached to the jumperoo toward her mouth so she can chew on it. Another tooth is trying to pop through, so she's been chewing on everything she can lately.

"Did you hear that, baby girl? Ry said I'm on baby duty." My voice grabs her attention, and she screeches at me in excitement. "Who's ready for a daddy day?" I ask her, walking over to take her out of the contraption. "That's right, baby girl, you are stuck with me all day." I nuzzle her neck, sucking in a deep breath of her clean skin. Unfortunately, she must have just filled her diaper because I get a nose full of the nastiest smell. "Good lord, kid, what is Riley feeding you?" I tease her, tickling her belly as I head for the nursery to change her diaper.

All I get is some babbles as I lay her down on the changing table. I get out everything that I'll need to take care of this biohazard. She's all smiles as I slip her shorts off and open her diaper up. I've become quite the pro at this changing diapers thing, something I never thought that I'd do in my life. "Good God, child. You are worse than some of the guys on the team, and that is saying something," I tease my daughter as I finish cleaning her up. Thankfully, she didn't blow her diaper out. She's done that a few times when in the jumper.

"What's going on in here?" Riley asks a few minutes later.

"This one decided that while you were in the shower, it was a good time to make Daddy change her biohazard-level diaper," I tell Riley from the floor where I'm sitting with Evie between my legs. We have a few toys between us as she works on getting stronger, sitting up on her own.

"Good girl!" Riley praises her. "Way to save the bad ones for Daddy," she says as she joins us on the floor. Evie flings herself toward Riley, obviously wanting to go to her. I'm sure, in her mind, Riley is her mom and the only motherly figure that she knows.

"Don't encourage her, she needs to save that crap for when I'm not around. I almost gagged it was so bad."

"Oh, so she should leave it for me?" she protests. "That doesn't seem very fair," she teases.

"Fine," I give in easily. "Are you ready to head outside?" I ask. With a full day off before I leave on another road trip tomorrow, we have some grand plans to just stay home today and spend the time together, only the three of us.

"Yep," Riley says, popping the p. "Already got my swimsuit on."

"Then what are we waiting for?" I ask as I hop up off the floor then offer my hand to Riley to pull her and Evie up. I lead them out to the backyard. Riley sets Evie down on a blanket with a few of her toys then joins her there. She rubs some sunblock all over Evie then does the same thing to herself.

"Here, let me help you," I offer, holding my hand out for the bottle of lotion. I pour some into my palm then rub both hands together. I rub it all over Riley's back, making sure to slip my fingertips underneath her bikini straps. They might not just slip under the straps; I take the liberty to move them past the cups, flicking her nipples.

"Justin," she warns. "Your daughter is right here," she reminds me, causing my dick to go a little soft.

"Fine, I'll be a good boy," I tell her as I pull my shirt off over my head. I'd also already put my trunks on earlier, so I'm ready for the pool. "Want to help me with my sunblock?"

"That depends..." she states, giving me a stern look.

"What?" I ask, pleading my innocence.

"Don't give me that look. You know exactly what," she says as she grabs the sunblock and puts a generous amount in her hand. "Roll over," she demands, and I do just that. I lay on my stomach on the blanket next to Evie. Riley straddles my ass, which, of course, does things to my dick. Her hands glide over my back, the muscles jumping under her touch. "You're a little jumpy today," she says as her hands rub the lotion into my skin.

"You would be, too, if you were in my position," I say into the blanket. I've got my head face down as I focus on taking in calm even breaths while she's torturing me with her hands.

"Dddddd," Evie babbles from next to me; she must teeter and lose her balance because, before I know it, she's laying across my head, drool dropping down onto my neck. I squirm, trying to move her and wipe the drool off of me.

Riley busts out laughing, hard enough that I can feel her shaking atop of me. I wrap an arm around Evie and then flip myself from under Riley in one quick move. I grab her mid flip so that I don't crush or hurt her while I'm moving. "You find that funny?" I ask, pulling her into me.

"I watched it all happen so fast, yet it felt like slow motion," she says between fits of giggles. "The way your body recoiled when the drool hit your neck was priceless."

She's still laughing hard as we lie here. Evie is facing out from my body but being held against it with one arm securing her to my side. "Get it out, babe, just remember that payback is a bitch."

"It's no worse than being peed on," she deadpans.

"I'd almost rather that. It felt so gross, which was made worse by it being a surprise," I tell her as Evie screeches again from my arms.

"Let's get into the pool; it looks like little miss, here, is ready," Riley points out as she heads to get into the pool. I walk around to the steps, easing my way into the water. With the sun already beating down on us and the summer heat well upon us, the coolness of the pool feels fantastic. As soon as Evie's feet hit the water, she starts kicking like she's a little fish. I wade out a bit, bobbing her along with me until I reach where Riley is standing, holding the baby float thing that she loves hanging out in. It works well and helps keep her occupied while we float around the water.

SIXTEEN
RILEY

"Okay, so you'll be back late Wednesday night, early Thursday morning, and your parents arrive on Friday. Do we want to plan on anything special while they're here?" I ask as Justin packs his suitcase for a three-night road trip.

"I don't think so, they don't usually require any fanfare when they come to see me, and we can all be honest, they aren't coming for me anymore."

"Oh, I'm well aware that they're only coming to get an Evie fix. Well, that and your mom is excited to see us together." I flash him a small smile.

"Yeah, she's reminded me of that fact no less than a hundred times," he deadpans as he rolls a few T-shirts before placing them into his bag. Once the shirts are in his bag, he leans over and drops a peck on the corner of my lips. I miss him when he's gone, but I find it fascinating to watch him pack so often. It's like second nature to him to have to pack all the time and head out. Such is the life of a professional athlete. Half of the season is spent on the road, and that's a shit ton of time when you really look at the schedule.

"Did you see the headline about you today?" I ask, not sure if he saw it or not, since it hasn't come up yet.

"Yeah," he grunts out. "I really hate that woman. She's a devil in sheep's clothing."

"I didn't get the greatest vibe from her, either," I tell him. I noticed that she did precisely what he warned me about and got close to the friends and family section so she could attempt to eavesdrop on what we were talking about. "I think it will only be a matter of days before they figure out who I am," I tell him, not really caring, but also knowing that my number one focus needs to be keeping Evie safe once they do, so if that means keeping her safely secured in the house, then I will.

"I agree. I was a little shocked that they haven't already, to be honest."

"I'm sure that they'll quickly figure out I'm Derek's sister and start making lots of assumptions."

"Yeah, like my nanny turned sex slave," he jokes, dropping a full kiss onto my lips.

"Don't be crass." I laugh against his lips as I smack my hands on his chest.

"Just telling the truth," he says before deepening the kiss. His fingers sink into my hair as his palms cup my cheeks. He angles my head precisely right, allowing him to deepen the kiss as he desires. I sink into him. Into this embrace, this kiss. By the time we break apart, my body is humming for more. More kissing. More touching. More of everything he is willing to give me.

"I'm going to miss you," I whisper as I place my head against his chest.

"I'm going to miss you, as well. Maybe my next road trip, you and Evie will have to come out with me."

"Maybe," I state. He's brought up the idea once before, but I never gave it much thought.

"Do you have any plans while I'm gone?" he asks as he zips up his suitcase.

"Not really, hanging out with Jillian and the kids. Probably take a few walks to the park, but otherwise just some lazy summer days."

"Just be careful while you're out and about. I don't want anyone harassing you while I'm not around to protect the two of you." His protectiveness of both Evie and me is downright sexy.

"Always," I assure him. "I'll always make Evie's security my priority. I love her as if she's my own daughter and would do anything to protect her."

"I just worry about both of you and know you'll do everything you can to keep her safe," he says, pulling his hat off and tossing it onto the bed next to me. He runs his hands through his hair, tugging at the ends slightly. "Fuck. I just worry that something's going to happen to one or both of you while I'm not here to do anything about it."

"Justin." I say his name to attempt to get his attention. I reach out and grab his hand. "We'll be good. If something were to happen, I'd get help. I have Jillian and some of the other WAGs that I'm sure I could call. Worst case scenario, I call the cops if it's something that serious."

"I know," he says, blowing out a huge breath. He shifts until he's standing between my thighs then cups my cheeks in his big hands. "I know you'll be fine; it's just me worrying. Not something that I'll probably ever stop doing. Becoming a father has changed me. I hope that you can see that. See that I'm no longer the guy I used to be, the playboy."

"You've definitely changed. I can't attest to the playboy times that much, but I'm also not complaining about what's standing in front of me."

"You're one of the best things to happen to me. I hope you know that," he says, then covers my lips with his own. I fall back onto the bed, pulling him with me. My legs wrap around his waist, pulling his dick against my center. I can feel him harden as I grind against him—no shame to my game. I can't get enough of him, and thankfully, it appears that he can't get enough of me. That first night that we slept together unleashed this almost uncontrollable desire that I have for Justin. The first few times were a little painful, but he was so gentle with me that it quickly gave way to pure pleasure. "You're feisty this afternoon," he says, kissing his way to my jaw, nipping at the skin between sucking kisses.

"Gotta take advantage of you while you're home," I somehow manage to get out as he drives me crazy. Between his mouth, wandering hand that has snaked under my shirt to tweak my nipple, while the other slides inside my yoga pants and is circling my clit, I'm ready to come apart at his hands.

"You're so fucking sexy when you're about to come," he

says, nipping at my neck a little harder. "The way your skin flushes," he pauses to suck my earlobe between his teeth, releasing it quickly, "the way your skin puckers in goose bumps after I rub my lips across it." His lips ghost along my collarbone, and up the other side of my neck, stopping shortly to suck at my pulse, that's pounding. "The way your pussy latches on to my fingers when I slide them inside you," he says as he does just that, and I cry out.

"Jus...tin!" I say, dragging his name out as I unravel at his doing.

He pulls his hand from my center, bringing his fingers to his mouth and sucking them clean. "I love the way you taste," he tells me.

"Mhmm..." I hum, enjoying the blissed state I'm in from that orgasm. "Want me to take care of that?" I ask him, reaching for his erection that's bulging in his shorts.

"Not going to deny you." He smirks at me as he reaches down to unzip his fly. I watch as he pulls his cock from his boxers, sliding them down his legs and out of the way—my mouth waters as he strokes his cock a few times. I shift on the bed until I'm lying directly in front of him in a position that I can suck his cock into my mouth. "Fuuuuuuuuuuuck!" he groans as I slide my tongue down the rigid underside of his hard shaft. I return to the tip, kissing it lightly before I suck him into my mouth, taking him in as far as I can. The tip hits the back of my throat, and I pull back until just the head remains. Hollowing my cheeks, I suck hard as I bob on his cock. Justin slides his hands into my hair. He doesn't fully take over, but I can feel the slight guidance that he gives me, showing me exactly what he wants and needs. I wrap my fist around the base of his shaft, stroking it up and down in rhythm with my mouth.

"I'm close..." he warns, tapping my cheek in a warning. I flick my eyes up towards his, making quick eye contact for just a second before I suck him into the very back of my throat. I gag slightly when his cock hits the back of my throat, but I breathe around it. I swallow around his cock, and at that moment, I feel him harden just as his orgasm hits him. Hot cum coats the back of my throat, and I swallow. "Fuck, baby. That's it, take my cock, suck it dry." His dirty talk spurs me on. I love it when he lets go in the moment. I never thought that I'd be a fan of some dirty sex talk, but damn does it make me wet.

I pop off his cock, and he wipes his thumb along my lips, helping to wipe away some of the extra fluids. "Damn," he says as he drops onto the bed next to me. I rest my head on his chest as we both bask in the aftermath.

Our relaxing only lasts a few minutes before Evie starts squawking over the baby monitor. "I'll get her," he says, pushing up from the bed. He quickly tucks his cock back into his boxers and shorts, then flashes me a quick wink before he ducks into the bathroom to wash up quickly. I follow suit, cleaning myself up before I join the two of them in the living room.

"Baseball's Bad Boy Turned Single Dad Isn't As Wholesome As He'd Like You To Believe"

I read the headline two more times, looking at the attached pictures. They sure don't look like the Justin that I've gotten to know the past couple of months. I have a hard time believing that he'd do this to me, to Evie. Two chicks are sitting on his lap, in a bar, where drinks litter the table in front of and beside them. One woman has her arm wrapped tightly around his neck, holding his face to her boobs, while the other is kissing his neck. My stomach rolls, and I have to breathe deep to not lose my breakfast.

I close out of the web browser and set my phone down. I don't need to read any more of that crap article. Not until I can talk to him and find out what the hell is going on while he's in Cleveland. What would possess him to go out like that? To cheat on me? I talked to him just before I fell asleep last night. He said that he was in his room for the night, planned to go to sleep as soon as we hung up. There has to be a reasonable explanation for this shit show.

"Good morning!" Jillian answers her phone on the first ring.

"Jill." My shaky voice gets her name out.

"Riley," she states my name, the tone of her voice changing from cheerful to all business. "What's wrong? Is everything okay with Evie? Are you okay?" She rapidly fires questions at me.

"There's an article with pictures," I say quietly. "From last night."

"Oh, hell no," she says. "Motherfluffer!" she whispers under her breath, censoring herself. "I'll call you back," she tells me then hangs up.

I don't really know what to think at this moment. I'm

trying to keep myself calm as I pace around the kitchen. Evie is in her highchair, eating some breakfast. I haven't even touched the cup of coffee I poured just before opening my phone to be assaulted by that article.

"Oh, Evie, girl. What has your daddy done?" I ask her as tears prick my eyes. My mind races as I debate if I should call him. What if the article is right and he's passed out somewhere with these two women? What am I going to do if he spent the night fucking them? I can't stop the tears, at this point, and I don't care to. Big fat tears roll down my cheeks, hitting the countertop as I let all of the emotions out. The one thing that I worried the most about is happening. How am I going to be able to stay here? Continue taking care of Evie, having to live with Justin? I'd fallen in love with him over the last couple of months, put my life in his hands, and now what do I have to show for it? A few thousand dollars in my bank account and a broken heart? It doesn't appear that I made a sage decision. Once again, I'm going to have to start over.

I wipe the tears from my cheeks, grabbing a tissue from the box and blowing my nose. The sound attracts Evie's attention and causes her to laugh at me. "You think that's funny?" I say to her before blowing again. Her belly laughs filling the air and causing me to laugh while I cry some more. What am I going to do without this little girl in my life all the time? I can't think of what my days will be like, not having her in them.

My phone rings, buzzing against the counter. I don't look at the screen before sliding my finger across it, bringing it to my ear. "Hello," I say, my voice still shaky.

"Riley, baby?" Justin's voice fills my ears and my heart drops to the floor, along with fresh new tears that I can't stop. "Please, baby, just listen," he pleads.

I clear my throat, straighten my spine, and with as much mirth as I can muster reply to him. "What?" I pause. "What the hell happened last night?"

"Nothing," he says, blowing out a huge breath. "That article is complete and utter bullshit. Those pictures are from another time, I don't really know when, but they definitely aren't from last night. Hell, they aren't even from this year," he tells me. "I promise you, Riley. I was not out at a bar last night, and I definitely wasn't with two women. I got off the phone with you, rolled over, and went to sleep."

"What?" I ask. I'm so confused. Confused by the article, confused about what to think or believe. He's never given me a reason to not believe him, so why would he lie now? "But why? Why would they print that? Post that picture?"

"Because they're trying to get a rise out of me, you, hell —anyone. I knew that bitch was up to no good after the family game last weekend and the article they ran the next day, but I didn't think she'd stoop this low," he growls. "The trashier the headline and the more believable they can make it appear, the more clicks they get. Derek is calling Carmen for me, to get them on it, as well as my own personal PR reps. The reporter that posted this will pay, mark my words."

"I..." I stammer, pausing to suck in a deep breath. My thoughts are still flying around my head a million miles a minute. One moment I thought that I'd lost the man I love, and the next, he's telling me everything that I thought I just learned was complete bullshit. "I'm sorry I freaked out and assumed the worst," I say to him as I shrink into myself. "I should have called you first and asked you about it before freaking out, but I didn't. I let it get to me. I believed it because of the picture," I tell him honestly, feeling like a complete bitch that I just jumped to the worst conclusion.

"Fuck!" Justin swears. I can tell that he's livid pissed right now. "I'm not mad at you, hurt a little that you'd even think I could do this to you... to us. But I get it. I don't have the best reputation. I lived it up in the past, and it's hard for some people to believe that I've changed. That I'm not all about the partying and sleeping around like I once was. I went from being a reporter's dream to a boring person in their eyes."

"If they only knew how not boring you are," I try and joke, hoping to lift the somber mood between the two of us.

"I think, once I'm home, we need to sit down and have a serious conversation. Don't think that this will be a one-time thing. People are vicious. They'll dig up shit from months or years ago and try and play it off like it was yesterday."

"That's now abundantly clear. When do you think that picture was taken?"

"Looking at it, probably last summer, if I had to guess. I recognize the bar, it's one here in Cleveland, so they at least got that much right. But I definitely haven't stepped foot into it this trip, so the last time it could have been was when we played here last summer."

I blow out a huge breath then fill my lungs with a calming one. My eyes close, and I repeat the breathing exercise again, feeling the tension and stress leaving my body. I feel tired and weak after that stressful half hour. So tired that I feel like I could go back to bed and sleep for hours. However, that isn't possible with a squawking baby that I'm in charge of today. "How's Evie?" Justin asks, breaking the silence that fell between the two of us as we both digested this morning's events.

"She's good. Just eating her breakfast and smiling at me," I tell him as I sit down on a chair in front of her. I grab the bowl of oatmeal I made for her, offering up a bite. She loves this stuff and starts to get excited about the next bite. "Want to see her?" I offer. We've gotten into the habit of FaceTiming while Justin is on the road. It's the only way that they can still bond while he's gone.

"Sure," he says. I hit the button to switch over to the video and prop my phone up on the table so that he can see both of us while I continue feeding her. "Ev-ie!" he sing-songs her name, and she looks around for him. She finally looks at the phone, and her face lights up when she sees him.

"Ddddd!" she stammers, my eyes go huge like saucers, and I look at her and then him.

"Did you just hear that?" he asks, a look of complete bliss filling his face.

"I did! I think she's trying to say her first word!" I cry out, cheering her on as new tears spring to my eyes. I'm such an emotional mess this morning. I must be about to start my damn period.

"I can't wait to hear it in person," he tells me, and I feel bad that he wasn't here to hear it himself.

"At least you heard it the first time. I won't have to lie to you when you do hear it and say that it was her first time."

"What, what other firsts have I really missed that you've just passed on and said it was her first time when I was able to catch it?" he asks, a playful yet stern look on his face.

"I plead the fifth," I tease him, fanning my innocence.

"Ry, don't be lying to me now."

"Okay," I give in. "She'd rolled over a few times while you were gone on a road trip before you saw it when you got back. I didn't want you to feel bad for missing it, so I just played it off as if that was her first time."

I give him a sorrowful look, attempting to apologize for doing so.

"I guess I'll forgive you, since you were doing it for a good reason, just don't keep doing it. I know I'm going to miss things. Just hazards of the job."

"Okay," I agree with him. "I'm sorry," I reiterate.

"What's on the agenda for today?" he asks, changing the subject.

"Not much. I think we're just going to hang around here. Maybe head up to the park this morning for a little bit. A storm is supposed to roll in this afternoon, so I want to be inside by then. Maybe we'll hunker down in the living room and watch you kick some butt today." I smile at him through the camera. My reflection looks horrible. I haven't showered, my eyes are all puffy and my face is all red and splotchy from crying, and my hair is in a rat's nest on the top of my head. I look like a mess.

"I wish I was there and could kiss you right now," Justin tells me.

I look down at myself, then back at him, raising my eyebrows at him. "I look like a hot mess."

"You look like a beautiful hot mess, one I'd still love to kiss right about now."

"You're incorrigible."

"Yet, you still love me," he says, stopping me in my tracks. We've never said that to one another outright.

I look him in the eyes. Well, as much as I can since we're seeing each other over a phone's camera. "Are you denying it?" he asks, lifting a brow in question.

"N-no," I stammer. "It's true. I do love you."

"That's the best thing I've heard all day, and a good thing, since I love you, too, Riley. So damn much," he tells me, and those damn tears are back. "I'm sorry I said it for the first time over a damn video call. Now I really wish I was there to pull you into my arms and kiss the daylight out of you."

"I know it wasn't conventional, but thank you anyway. I think after this morning, I needed to hear those words. I needed that affirmation."

"I know, baby. But please, *please*, promise me that if something like this happens again, and I'm sure it will, that you'll come to me first before you let it get to you or before you believe one single thing the tabloids post about me, you, or us."

"I promise," I tell him, and mean it with everything that I am.

"Ddddd!" Evie squawks again, hitting her hand against the highchair. I realize I got caught up in talking to Justin and stopped feeding her, so I give her another bite of the oatmeal.

"You be good, baby girl," Justin says to her. She looks at the camera again and babbles at him some more. He just soaks up these precious moments, even if they are through the phone. "All right, my two favorite girls, I've got to get going. We've got a team meeting before a light pre-game workout. I'll call you once we're done and on the bus back to the airport. I can't wait to have you in my arms again tonight," he tells me, flashing me a devilish grin.

"Only if you're lucky!"

"Bye, I love you," he says, laughing at me as the connection ends.

Evie squawks at me once again, telling me how unimpressed she is with my lack of feeding her. "So sorry," I tell her as I get another spoonful ready for her.

Once she's finished with breakfast, I take her in for a bath. Now that she's eating actual food and not just drinking bottles, she's quite messy after most meals, and it's just easier to wash her down quickly.

With a clean baby, I get her dressed in a cute summer outfit that I pulled from one of the bins that Jillian passed down. It's got little fruit slices all over it and ruffles on her butt. Ruffles make everything better. "How about some jumperoo time so I can shower?" I ask her as I set her down on the floor of my bedroom with a few toys so that I can go grab it and bring it into my bathroom.

She babbles and laughs the entire time I'm in the shower and getting dressed. I pull on a pair of cutoff shorts, a Lightning tank top that JJ brought home for me not long ago, and my Berk sandals. After brushing my hair out, I pull it up and into a bun on the top of my head. Between the heat and humidity, I hate it being on my neck all day.

"Shall we go to the park, Evie girl?" I ask her as I take her out of the jumper. She kicks her legs in excitement as I place her on my hip. I take her out to the garage, securing her in the stroller before heading out.

"How are you?" Jill asks in lieu of a greeting as I answer her call.

"I'm good, we're good. It was all just a bunch of nothing. That picture was from last summer sometime, and he wasn't at the bar last night. Just some trashy reporter was trying to start shit," I tell her in a quick recap of the morning. "What are you and the girls up to?"

"Just hanging out. They've been bugging me to go do something. They want out of the house."

"Evie and I are on our way to the park if you want to come join us," I offer.

"You know, we might just do that. Meet you there in ten?"

"Sounds good, see you then," I tell her before hanging up the call. I set my phone in the cup holder and keep on moving. We arrive at the park a few minutes later, finding it a little busy this morning. I guess we weren't the only ones with the idea to get in some park time before the storm rolls in later today.

I park the stroller and take Evie out. There's a baby swing open, and those are her favorite. So, we head over to it while we wait for Jillian and the girls to arrive.

"Hello," a young woman pushing a baby a little bigger

than Evie greets me as I start pushing her. "Your baby is so cute."

"Oh, thanks! She's not mine, I'm the nanny," I tell her.

"Me too!" she tells me, a little excited. "How old is she?"

"Six, almost seven months. How about your little one?" I ask, making polite conversation.

"He just turned eight months old yesterday," she says, pushing him again. "I'm Brooke, by the way."

"Riley, and this is Evie," I introduce both of us.

"This little chunk is Benjamin."

"He sure is a cutie. How long have you been his nanny?" I ask.

"Since he was about six weeks old. Both of his parents are doctors, so they have some crazy hours. How about you?"

"Since she was about three months old," I tell her, not divulging anything about who her parents are.

"It's so fun, isn't it?" Brooke asks.

"It is. Especially since she's such an easy baby." We both get distracted by the babies for a few moments. "Is this your only nanny job?" she asks.

"Yep, I live with her family," I tell her, still being vague. "It was a bit of an urgent situation, and I'd just moved here when the need came up. Her dad and my brother are best friends, so it worked out perfectly for everyone involved."

"Oh, nice. I found Benjamin's parents from my prior nanny family. I used to watch his cousins, but they're now all school age and didn't need me anymore. About that time, Benjie came along, and I made the transition."

"Sounds like it was meant to be," I tell her, smiling at

Benjamin. He's giggling as he swings back and forth, Evie matching his excitement from her swing.

"We finally made it," Jillian says, stopping next to me.

"Oh, good," I tell her, looking around for the girls. "Where are my nieces?" I ask when I can't find them.

"Over on the slide," she says, pointing at the climbing structure. "Hi, I'm Jillian," she introduces herself to Brooke.

"Brooke, this is my sister-in-law." I quickly introduce the two of them.

"Nice to meet you." They trade pleasantries before we all get distracted once again by the kids.

"Auntie Ry!" Penelope runs up to me a few minutes later.

"Hey, Penny girl." I greet her as she runs into my outstretched arms as I crouch down to her level. I stand up, her arms wrapped around my neck, and my arms wrapped around her torso in a bear hug. "How are you today?" I ask her, placing a kiss on her cheek before I set her back down.

"I's good. Can you come over for lunch?" she asks.

"Probably," I tell her. "Can Evie take a nap in your room if we come over?"

"Yes!" she says before running off to play again.

"I guess we're coming over for lunch," I tell Jillian.

"Sounds good. I was going to invite you over anyway."

"Or we could go out somewhere and then back to watch some movies while it storms," I suggest. "No cooking or clean up required."

"Now, that sounds like the perfect plan," she says, then takes off to go check on Addison, who's calling her over.

"Your niece is such a cutie," Brooke says, pulling my attention back to her.

"Thanks, they're both pretty great, if I do say so myself."

"Kind of nice to have them so close by," she comments.

"It is. Jillian stays home with them, and my brother's work schedule makes him gone a lot, so it works well for us to get together throughout the week. They love playing with Evie, almost like a warm-up for when their brother is born this fall."

"How fun. I was going to ask when she was due but didn't want to be rude," she says, smiling at me.

"Yeah," I say, laughing. "The first boy, so we're all excited about that."

"I bet. Do you have any other nieces?"

"Nope, just my brother and me."

"Fun. I love being an aunt. Unfortunately, I don't live near my siblings anymore, so I don't get to see them and spoil them all that often. I moved out here with a previous nanny family."

"That's cool. I take it you like it here, then?"

"I do! I've been here now for about six years, and it really became home. You said you'd just moved here before starting to nanny, is that correct?"

"Yep, I finished my degree last year, but my first job was kind of a crash and burn. Nothing was really holding me to Ohio, so I asked my brother and sister-in-law if they'd be okay with me moving here to be close to them, and they loved the idea. So that weekend, I packed my things and drove down. A few weeks after that, the need for a last-minute nanny came up, and I hadn't secured a job yet, so it worked perfectly."

"Sounds like it was meant to be, then. Was her previous nanny just not a good fit?" she asks.

"Nope, just a last-minute need," I tell her, being as vague as possible.

"Well, I'm glad it worked out, then."

"Me too," I tell her, smiling slightly at how well things have worked out.

Evie starts crying, I think she's tired of swinging, for now. I pull her out of the swing, holding her up as if she's an airplane, bringing her down so I can blow a raspberry on her chubby cheek, then back up again. We repeat this a few times until I've got her laughing hard.

"It was nice talking to you, Brooke; maybe we'll see you and Benjamin down here again."

"Nice to meet you, Riley! Would you like to exchange numbers? We could make a plan to meet up sometime?"

"Sure," I tell her, grabbing my phone from my back pocket as I place Evie on my hip. I enter Brooke's number then shoot her a text, so she has mine. "Evie and I look forward to it!" I tell her before I walk off to find Jillian and the girls. I take Evie down the slide a couple of times, then head for the stroller and pull out a blanket to spread out on the grass so we can sit down. I pull out a few of her toys, and she happily plays in the shade.

"Ugh. Don't ever get pregnant at the beginning of the year," Jillian says as she lowers herself to the ground. "Being as large as a house in the middle of summer is miserable."

"No plans of getting pregnant anytime soon," I tell her, holding back a laugh.

"I'm serious. When you are ready for a baby of your own, not that Evie isn't basically yours already, try to plan to get pregnant during the summer. That way, you're big when it's wintertime and not so godforsaken hot outside. The only nice thing about being pregnant during the summer is the baby will be born towards the end of the season, hopefully, so Derek will be home a lot while he's little, and I'll need the most help."

"I'll try and keep that in mind," I tell her, just to appease her.

"You and JJ going to be okay?" she asks quietly.

"I think so. I promised him that I wouldn't jump to conclusions if it happens again. It was just hard to see and read."

"It is. Hopefully, they'll get over making him into a headline. But from experience, it still hurts every time it happens. Even when you know that not one ounce of it is the truth. Derek has had his fair share of headlines, and so many of them were completely made up shit just to make him look bad and for them to get clicks to their website. The best advice that I can give you is to stop looking at them. Don't go searching for what they're posting. If it isn't in the forefront of your mind, then it can't put that little bit of doubt there, either. You either have to trust him one thousand percent, or not. There isn't any place for doubt of that kind if you want things to work between the two of you."

"I know. I like your advice to not go looking for articles.

It's just hard sometimes, ya know," I tell her as I hand a toy back to Evie.

"Oh, do I ever," she says, laughing. "When Derek first started playing here, I had a Google alert set to send me anything his name was mentioned in. I had to turn it off within the first week. At that point, he wasn't making the news for anything scandalous, but I realized even then that people would write whatever they wanted to, no matter how true it was or how far they were bending that truth."

"That's so shitty. Why is it that they can post complete crap and get away with it?"

"Free speech and all that jazz. Things like this morning's post, JJ's PR company can get taken down and, in some instances, get them to issue an apology stating that it was incorrect information yada, yada, yada. While I appreciate those kinds of statements, it doesn't change the fact that they released that out there, and people aren't just going to forget about it. And nothing ever fully goes away once it's on the internet. And these shitty tabloids know that and bank on that for future articles. They want people to believe that these guys are just out partying it up while they're on the road, and it isn't like that doesn't happen. But they want to make it appear that everyone on the team is doing that, no matter if they have a wife and or kids back home. I won't lie to you and say that there hasn't been a married guy who has done just that, because they absolutely have, but it's not the everyday norm. Most of these guys are some of the sweetest, most down to earth, family men that you'll meet. They just happen to hit a ball for a living and get paid damn well to do so."

"I'm so glad that I have you to help me navigate all of this."

"And I'm here whenever you need me," she assures me.

"Thanks," I tell her, leaning over to give her a side hug.

"Ready to round up the kids and head out for some lunch? I'm starving."

"Sure. What does little mister want today?" I ask, nodding toward her stomach.

She rubs her stomach and laughs. "Tacos sounds really good right now."

"They do. Qdoba?" I suggest.

"That'll do," she agrees.

"Okay, you stay here with this little chunk, and I'll go round up the girls," I tell her as I pop up from the ground. It only takes me a minute or so to spot the girls and get them over to the blanket. "Did you guys walk here or drive?" I ask Jillian as I fold up the blanket and stuff it in the bottom basket of the stroller.

"We drove. I didn't want to tire out with the heat."

"Sounds good. Do you want to follow me home so I can grab the car seat and then we can head out?"

"We can do that," Jillian agrees. "You can get a head start, and I'll get the girls loaded up, and then we'll be over in just a few."

"Perfect. I'll see you three in just a few, then," I tell her as Evie and I head off toward home.

"Hell of a game," Matt O'Riley, our first baseman, says, smacking my ass with his glove.

"Hell yes, it was," I tell him, repeating the ass slap.

"You get everything straightened out from this morning?" he questions.

"Yep. Carmen was on it, so was my PR rep. I got a text this afternoon that they got the website to take it down and issue an apology. Those fuckers know the damage is already done."

"Do you know who posted it?" he asks.

"Yeah, that chick reporter from that sports blog. She was at the family day game, asking lots of questions, trying to weasel her way into the friends and family area, as well. She rubbed me wrong with some of the questions she was asking down on the field and then her little article the next morning."

"Sounds like she's got her sights locked on to you and just wants to bring you down. You didn't fuck her in the past only to kick her out of your bed, did you? Maybe she's out for personal revenge?" he suggests.

"Fuck, no." I balk at that idea, but the truth is, that exact situation could have happened; although I usually remember the women I've fucked in the past. The number isn't quite as high as some of my teammates assume it is.

"Maybe one of her friends?" he asks.

"Hell if I know. She might just be a crazy chick that has a vendetta, for whatever reason. Mad that she can't bag a professional athlete."

"Maybe. Well, hopefully, she backs off your ass."

"Maybe someone else on the team could fuck up and give her a new focus," I joke.

"Not it," he says, touching the tip of his nose like kids do when they don't want to be the one to have to do something sacrificial.

"Your time will come," I tell him.

"Nope. I'm an altar boy," he says, and I bust up laughing at his lie.

"I wouldn't believe that for a minute," I retort.

"Hey, we can't all be reformed manwhores like you," he tosses right back at me as we both start to strip out of our uniforms.

I quickly drop everything, wrapping a towel around my waist, then grab my shower kit from my locker before heading in to do my business. Visitor locker rooms are never all that fancy, just the basic necessities. Sometimes we're lucky to have enough hot water and good water pressure for everyone to get through showers after the game.

Once I'm back at my locker, I quickly pull on a pair of

boxer briefs before running my towel over my head to dry off my hair. I pull out my cell to see if I have any missed messages or calls and see a few notifications from Riley, so I unlock my phone, going directly to her messages.

First, I find a couple of pictures from Riley playing with Evie, Addison, and Penelope. Those are followed by one of my girls curled up together on the couch, bottle in Evie's hands and mouth as Riley's lips are pressed against the top of her head. She's captioned the image with "Go, Daddy! Your girls are cheering you on!" I can't help but smile at the image and message that came in around when the game would have started. Two more pictures follow that awhile later, one of Evie passed out in Riley's arms, with the caption "Someone couldn't hack staying awake for the entire game." The fact that she fell asleep doesn't surprise me one bit, nor would Riley want her to. She's worked hard on getting Evie into a good solid routine, and sleep is an essential part of that.

Her final picture causes my eyebrows to pop up. She sent it just a few minutes ago, probably while I was in the shower. It's a good thing none of the other guys are close enough to see over my shoulder right about now. This picture is meant just for my eyes and has my dick stirring in my boxers. Not something that I really want popping up while in the locker room, but my girl is sexy as fuck. She's standing in my bedroom in front of the full-length mirror I have on the closet door, my jersey on, only one button holding it together between her breasts, showing me slivers of the bra and panties she's got on underneath. "I'll be waiting for you..." she captioned it, capped off with a kissing emoji. My mouth waters at the fact that I know *exactly* what is waiting for me when we get home late tonight.

"What's got you so engrossed in your phone?" Derek asks, smacking me on the shoulder. I quickly lock my phone, setting it down on the shelf in my locker.

"Just some pictures from Riley from their day," I tell him, having to clear my throat thanks to that last one.

"Fuck, my sister better not be sending you nudes," he grumbles.

"Fuck no. Some not suitable for your or anyone else's eyes, maybe," I tease him, and he just groans.

"Why do you have to say that shit to me? It's bad enough that I know that you're fucking her."

"Then, don't ask," I reply, shooting him a shit-eating smirk. In all reality, Derek has taken the news of Riley and me pretty well. I was expecting him to kick my ass, but one conversation over beers, and he was willing to accept that we were serious about each other. I know that he wouldn't hold back kicking my ass if I was to ever hurt her in any way.

"She over the drama from earlier? When I talked to Jillian, she said they'd had a good day together."

"Yeah, I got her calmed down. I just hope it doesn't happen again," I tell him honestly as I pull my shirt on over my head.

"We all know that won't happen anytime soon," he tells me, flashing me a sorrowful look. "Hell, as much as I don't want them posting anything about anyone on our team, I have to say, I'm thankful it isn't another thing about me, for once. About damn time someone else takes the spotlight from me."

"I'll gladly give it back or pass it on to someone else."

"I don't see that happening anytime soon," he quips.

I flip him the bird as I pack my things all away in my bag. I sling it over my shoulder and head out to the waiting bus that will take us to the airport. Once in my seat, I pull my phone back out and shoot off a text to Riley.

JJ: You still awake?

Riley: Yep

JJ: Thank you for *all* the pictures today… although, your brother almost caught me looking at that last one.

Riley: Oh god… maybe you should delete it.

JJ: Fuck, no. I'm keeping that one. That's spank bank material.

Riley: :groan:

Riley: Can you put it somewhere safe, at least? Fingerprint protect it? I DO NOT need my brother to find that in your camera roll.

Riley: I'm serious. I should have never sent it.

:smacking face:

JJ: Calm down, babe. It isn't like you're naked. But if it makes you feel any better, I'll figure out how to make sure it is locked down. I can research it on the flight home.

Riley: Thank you. I'll see what I can find, myself, and send it to you.

JJ: I'm not worried about it, babe. It isn't like the guys routinely flip through pictures on my phone.

Riley: Still.

JJ: Stop stressing. I want you nice and relaxed when I get home tonight. Can I wake you up when I get back?

Riley: That depends.......

JJ: On?

Riley: How do you plan on waking me up? :devilish grin emoji:

JJ: How does my mouth on your pussy sound?

Riley: Like the best way to be woken up.

JJ: Followed by you riding my cock. I want to see those tits bounce while you ride me.

Riley: Well, okay, then. (Also, I'm already wet thinking about it.)

JJ: Fuuuuuuuck. You had to go there, didn't you?

Riley: You painted such a vivid picture. Sorry that my body responded? :winky face – water droplets – winky face:

JJ: You're making me hard. Thank god I'm on the bus and not still in the locker room. That was a little awkward earlier when I first looked at the picture. Standing only a few feet from your brother with my dick going hard while I looked at your sexiness was throwing my mind for a loop.

Riley: #sorrynotsorry :shrugging shoulders:

JJ: You'll pay for that later. I can promise you that.

Riley: Promise?

JJ: Absolutely. :kissy-face emoji:

Riley: BRB... Evie is crying.

JJ: She okay? This is kind of a weird time of night
for her to be waking up, isn't it?

I flip out of my messages and start researching how to secure the pictures, for her sanity. Before I know it, the bus is moving, and we're off to the airport. The ballpark here in Cleveland isn't super far from the airport, and the flight is a quick one, less than an hour from wheels up to wheels down, so I'll be home and sliding into bed with Riley within two hours, max.

We arrive at the airport and I get settled. Most guys have a preferred seat or general area they like. Derek takes the seat across from me in our four-seat pod. Two of the seats face the back of the plane while the other two face forward like normal. There's a table in the center that we'll often play cards on during long flights.

Once settled, our flight attendant, Julie, makes her rounds, bringing us all drinks and any snacks that we might want. The team doesn't skimp when it comes to stocking the plane. I pull my phone out of my pocket, plugging it into the charger here at my seat—another perk of flying on a private jet. Riley still hasn't replied to my text after she went to deal with Evie, and that's starting to worry me.

"What's that look for?" Derek asks.

"I was texting with Riley on the bus, and she had to go as Evie was crying. She hasn't texted back, and I'm worried now that something is wrong."

"I'm sure everything is fine. Maybe she fell asleep lying down with her? Or maybe she's up with a new tooth pushing through?" he suggests.

"Maybe. I just wish she'd send me anything to tell me what's going on."

"Chill, bro. She's got it all under control," he tells me sternly. I know he's right, but it still doesn't change the fact that I don't know what is going on, so my mind starts racing and thinking of all that could go wrong.

Riley: Sorry for the delay. Everything is fine. She just needed to be cuddled for a few minutes to fall back to sleep. I think falling asleep in my arms earlier messed up her bedtime routine. Then I got sucked into cleaning the kitchen and starting the dishwasher. Forgot to check my phone until now.

JJ: I'm not going to lie; you had me panicking that something was wrong.

Riley: Sorry, didn't mean to. How long until you get home?

JJ: We're about to go wheels up, so just over an hour.

Riley: I'll be ready and waiting. :winky face:

JJ: Naked??

Riley: You'll just have to wait and see.

JJ: Fucking tease

Riley: Only for you

JJ: Damn right

Riley: I'm going to go soak in the tub for thirty or so minutes. Be nice and ready for you when you get here.

JJ: Fuuuuck. You did it again. I'm hard as a bat now. Thanks.

Riley: I'll gladly take care of that when you get here.

JJ: Damn right you will

Riley: :bring it gif:

Riley: Ok, I'm stripping and slipping into the bath now. I'll talk to you when you get home.

I internally groan at the mental images flashing through my mind. Riley can be such the little vixen; sometimes she does it on purpose, and sometimes she has no idea. I'm confident tonight is on purpose. A way for her to make sure I'm ready to pounce when I get home.

EIGHTEEN
RILEY

I slip beneath the hot water, the bath bomb I tossed in filling the room with a relaxing mixture of lavender and vanilla. I relax back against the tub, the angle is perfect for soaking. I can feel the water relaxing my muscles. I close my eyes and let the rest of the stress from today just melt away. I didn't realize just how much the events from this morning wore me out emotionally. I still can't believe that I jumped to the worst-case scenario. I should have never done that. I know it hurt Justin's feelings that I did, and I can understand why. I either trust him or I don't, and I didn't show the trust I do have very well. I let the lies lead me astray, which was the point of the stupid article.

I push all thoughts of it out of my mind. It is in the past. It wasn't true, and there's no reason to continue to dwell on it. I made a mistake, but it's time to move on and not let it continue to fester in my mind. We both learned something from it today, and I'm focusing now on not allowing it to repeat itself and learning from it as we move forward. To hear Justin tell me he loves me after all of that about blew me away. I didn't even care that he told it to me over the video call. Hearing those three sweet words leave his lips was like a calming balm to my fractured soul.

A smile tugs at my lips as I think about our text exchange from earlier. My sex starts to pulse, just thinking about what he plans to do to me when he returns. If there's one thing I've learned since we started dating it's the man has an incredible amount of stamina, and he's incredible at making my body come alive. I hate to think of anyone that came before me, but I can only thank all that experience he's got for the fantastic orgasms that he plies me with night after night.

I slip my hand down my torso, circling around my clit once my fingertips are low enough. I'm already strung tight, ready to come undone at the slightest touch. I imagine my fingers are his as I tease myself. I slip two fingers inside my pussy until I find that sensitive patch inside. I slide my fingertips along it until I feel myself start to spasm around my fingers.

I suck my bottom lip between my teeth, biting down to keep from yelling out with my orgasm. My fingers slip out as my body goes limp, all those lovely orgasmic hormones flooding my bloodstream.

I stay in the bath until the water starts to go tepid. I pull the plug and stay in the water until it's almost all drained out. I stand up and turn the shower on, rinsing off from the bath bomb. The hot water keeps my muscles nice and relaxed.

I lazily get out, drying off and slathering some lotion on before brushing my teeth. I'd pulled my hair up into a bun to keep it out of the water, so I let it back down, the light waves cascading down around my shoulders.

I slip between the sheets naked, just as I know Justin is hoping I'll be when he gets home soon. I pull my Kindle out from the nightstand, pulling up my newest book. I get lost in the pages over the next twenty or so minutes before the alarm system being turned off catches my attention. I hear it beep again, knowing that he's set it now that we're all inside.

I listen carefully to his movement through the house. I imagine him setting his bag down just inside the garage door where he'd stop to punch in his code. I hear his feet coming down the hall, then the light sound of a door opening as he pokes his head in to check on Evie. It melts my heart just how much he loves his daughter and how well he's adjusted to having her in his life. A minute later, he's pushing open the door to his room. I only have a bedside lamp on, set at its lowest setting.

JJ's gaze finds mine, his eyes adjusting to the low amount of light in the room. I can feel his eyes on me like a brand. I watch him as he looks up and down my form under only the sheet. The primal look of desire filling his eyes, even from this distance, has my body already aching for his touch.

After closing the door with a soft click, he closes the distance between the door and the bed. His fingertips graze up my body, starting about mid-calf and on top of the sheet. Even with the material between us, I can feel the heat from his fingers. "You're awake, guess I won't be waking you up with my mouth on your clit."

"Would you like me to pretend to be asleep?" I ask, my sass coming out strong tonight.

He chuckles, and I can feel those vibrations in my core. "Oh, sweetheart," he says, running his fingertips along my cheek before they pass over my bottom lip. "No pretending will be happening in this room tonight. Just you, me, and every dirty, delicious thing I can think of to put our bodies through," he tells me before he braces each of his arms on either side of me as his mouth claims mine in one hell of a demanding kiss. His tongue presses into my mouth as he takes complete control, not that I am fighting him for it tonight. I do not mind playing submissive to him, I trust him to never do something that would hurt me.

"Hmmm, you are naked," he hums against my lips. "My favorite way to find you in my bed," he tells me as he stands up again and quickly strips until he is naked himself. I watch as he palms his cock, giving it a few strokes. I lick my lips just thinking about sucking him deep into my throat. I love the power that it gives me to feel him come undone and knowing that I am the one doing that to him. It is a rush I never expected to feel until I experienced it with Justin.

"What are you going to do about it?" I ask him. His hand ghosts down my body, now exposed as he pushed the sheet out of the way. He grabs hold of my hips and maneuvers my body until my ass is on the edge of the bed. He sinks down to his haunches and throws my legs over his shoulders, his mouth quickly descending onto my center. The wicked things he does with his tongue have my body singing his praises as I arch off the bed. He releases my clit, and I cannot help but whimper at the loss of stimulation. I was on the edge of coming, but he has purposely backed off my orgasm, I am sure of it. "Don't tease me," I whine.

"I'll tease you all I want," he says, dragging the tip of his tongue from my opening, up my slit, and around my clit.

"Fuck!" I call out. "Do that again," I instruct, and thank the lord he actually listens to my request. He follows it up by slipping two fingers inside me, stretching me as he plunges his fingers in and out. I can hear as his fingers slide around, thanks to how wet I am. I am a little surprised that my body is strung so tightly, especially after my bath orgasm.

"That's it, baby, give it to me," he coaxes as he builds me right back up to the edge. This time he does not back off. He continues to fuck my pussy with two fingers as he sucks my clit again between his lips, flicking it relentlessly until I am screaming his name out, my legs clamping around his head. He wastes no time, pulling his fingers from me and reaching for a condom, rolling it on quickly before thrusting into me until he is balls deep.

"Yes!" I cry out in ecstasy.

"Fuck, you feel good," Justin grunts as he thrusts at an erratic pace, not letting up even with my body spasming around his cock. He latches on to my neck, sucking hard, hard enough that I'm sure he'll leave a hickey mark. "Shit!" he growls in my ear. "I'm going to come," he says as he thrusts one last time before I can feel him filling the condom. He stills above me, his forehead resting on the bed just above my shoulder. His body is trembling as he sucks in deep breaths. I can feel the pounding of his heart against my chest, and it matches my own erratic heartbeat.

"Welcome home," I whisper once I have caught my own breath and started to come down from my release high.

"Fuck, I'll leave more often if this is the welcome I get when coming home." He chuckles then kisses my temple. "I love you," he says sweetly before brushing his lips over mine.

His words settle into my heart, stitching that little crack that formed this morning. The one that I brought upon myself, but nonetheless needed stitching back together, and this man was exactly what I needed. My center clenches around his semi-hard cock that is still deep inside me. His words have me ready to go again.

Without words, he pulls out, and I whimper at the loss. He pulls off the used condom and goes to reach for another one. "Don't," I boldly tell him, reaching for his hand. "I don't want anything between us, not now, not ever."

"Are you sure?" he asks, stroking his cock a few times as he watches me closely.

"Positive. I love you, and you love me. Make love to me, Justin."

"Yes, ma'am," he says before motioning for me to move up the bed. He follows me up the center. Once I am settled, he places a kiss just above my center then kisses his way up my body. Nipping and sucking his way slowly, finally reaching my breasts, where he sucks one nipple then the other into his mouth, all while rolling the other between his fingertips. By the time he reaches my lips, I am on fire and ready for whatever he has planned next.

He pulls my left leg up and over his hip, lines his cock up with my entrance, and slowly pushes in. He watches as his cock disappears inside of me, only to pull out and do it again. The slowness drives me fucking insane. The feel of his cock bare and inside of me is intoxicating. "You feel amazing," he tells me, starting to slowly speed up his thrusts. I pull his face to mine, plunging my tongue into his mouth until we are so completely lost in each other that we both fall apart and over the orgasm cliff together.

Justin rolls off me, taking me with him as he does so. I can feel his release start to slide out of me, and it is such a weird feeling. I have obviously never had sex without a condom since this is our first time doing so. "Let me get you a towel to clean up with," he says, kissing my cheek before he gets up to grab one from the bathroom. He comes back a moment later, a warm wet washcloth in his hand. He gently wipes everything up then tosses the towel toward the laundry basket, missing it entirely as it plops onto the floor.

He hovers over me, locking his eyes with mine. The silent conversation flowing between the two of us right now has tears springing to my eyes.

"Why the tears, baby?" he whispers, breaking the silence between us.

"They're good tears," I tell him. "This just all feels so big and important."

"It is," he agrees with me, dropping his lips back to mine. "No one else I'd rather do this with. Thank you for being by my side, being my backbone when I needed one the most. Everything that you do to take care of Evie and me, I could never repay you for that. The way that you love her unconditionally, as if she was your own. That means more to me than you'll ever know."

"I do love her, both of you," I tell him, pressing a kiss to the corner of his mouth. He lies on his side, propped up with one arm. He cups my cheek with his other hand, wiping at the tears sliding down.

"We should get some sleep. It's been one long-ass day."

"I agree. I'm exhausted, especially now," I tell him, snuggling into his side once he's settled into his spot on the bed. "Love you," I whisper just before I fade off to sleep.

NINETEEN
JUSTIN

I WAKE UP TO AN EMPTY, COLD BED AND SUN SHINING in through the windows. I pull on some clean boxers and shorts after using the bathroom, and make my way out to the kitchen, where I find my two favorite girls dancing around as Riley waits for the coffee to brew and an egg to cook she has on the stove. I stand back, lean against the doorframe, and just watch the two of them.

If I were a stranger looking in the windows, I would never guess that I was not looking in on a mother and her daughter. It makes me hurt slightly for Evie that she does not have the opportunity to have this kind of bond with her birth mother. But on the other hand, the relationship that she has with Riley is special, all in its own right.

"Holy shit, you scared me," Riley exclaims as she spins around and sees me. The move makes Evie laugh and kick her legs in excitement. She sees me, and her entire face lights up.

"Hey, baby girl," I greet her, closing the distance

between us. I reach out and take Evie from Riley's arms as she leans for me at the same time.

"Dadadada..." she babbles, and I drink it all in, kissing her cheeks.

"That's right, Evie. Dada is home," I say, blowing a raspberry in the crook of her neck. She flings her head back as she laughs. Her little chubby hands rub my cheeks as she moves in to try and bite my nose. "Don't bite Daddy," I tell her firmly.

"Dadada," she screeches once again, and I can't help but laugh at her excitement.

"How are you this morning?" I ask Riley, tugging her closer to me so I can kiss the corner of her mouth.

"Good." She flashes me a sweet smile before turning back to her breakfast on the stove. The toaster pops up at that moment, shocking Evie in my arms.

"Has she eaten yet?" I ask as I walk over to the highchair.

"Nope, I was waiting until my food was done so we could eat at the same time. Do you want to feed her?"

"Yep. What's for breakfast today?" I ask Evie.

"I've got oatmeal and some banana I was going to cut up in small pieces for her. She really likes trying to pick up little pieces and feed herself. Now, if those bites actually make it into her mouth, is another story," Riley tells me. "Do you want some breakfast?" she asks as she plates her toast and egg.

"I can make something in a little bit. Sit and eat while your food is hot."

"Okay," she says as she pours a cup of coffee and grabs

her plate to join us at the table. I stir Evie's oatmeal together and cut up the banana Riley had peeled and ready.

"Open up!" I tell Evie as I zoom in the first bite of oatmeal like the spoon is an airplane. She excitedly kicks her legs and smacks the tray of her highchair with her hands as the spoon gets closer to her mouth. I sneak it in, successfully getting it all into her mouth.

The next ten or so minutes pass by in the exact same way. I feed Evie her entire breakfast, stopping when she wants to attempt to get a bite of banana into her mouth. It is quite comical to watch her smear it all over her face sometimes, and then how proud she is when she gets it into her mouth.

"What's on the agenda for today?" Riley asks once she is finished with her breakfast.

"I've got the entire day off, so I'm at your disposal."

"Mhmm," she hums, winking at me.

"Not around the baby," I joke, attempting to cover Evie's eyes. "I need to get in and get my hair cut, but besides that, I'm at your mercy."

"I was thinking of a walk to the park, maybe before lunch and naptime. While Evie's napping, you can go get your hair cut. Then maybe we can get together with Derek and Jillian for dinner?"

"Sounds like the perfect family day," I say and see how she stiffens slightly. *Shit, does she not see that is precisely what we are becoming?*

"I agree!" she says, quickly allowing that apprehensiveness to roll off.

"Let me text my guy and see if he can get me in this

afternoon, then," I tell her, grabbing my phone and shooting off the text.

"Are you ready?" I call into the bedroom, where Riley is just finishing up getting ready for the day. I took over baby duty, allowing her to go shower by herself without having to rush while Evie played in the jumperoo inside the bathroom. I got her all cleaned up from the mess she made at breakfast and dressed for the day. With Daddy dressing her, I make sure her shirt is one of the many that proclaim her as a daddy's girl.

"Almost!" she calls back. I put the sandals on Evie's feet that Riley picked out for her a few weeks ago.

"Ready for the park, baby girl?" I ask my daughter as I hold her up over my head as if she is a helicopter. All I get in return are some slobbery, smiles.

I love how lively she is starting to get. How much her little personality is coming out as every day passes. It still boggles my mind how Erica could just give this up. She still hasn't tried to contact me, and I have to wonder if she ever will. Once the courts awarded me with full custody, I worried less that she would just swoop in as quickly as she did before, but this time to try and take her from me.

"I'm ready," Riley says as she joins us in the living room. I take my time looking up her long, exposed legs. She has on a pair of chucks, shorts, and a tank top that shows off just a hint of cleavage. Enough to make my mouth water and my dick take notice.

"Let's go, then!" I clear my throat then stand to walk out to the garage. I put Evie in the stroller then grab Riley's hand as we head out.

We make it to the park and find it busier than I would have expected for a Thursday. Riley pulls Evie out of the stroller and beelines it for the swings. I stand a few feet back and just watch the two of them smiling and laughing together as she pushes the swing. The look of complete elation on Evie's face has me smiling right along with them.

I tug my ball cap a little lower as I notice people taking note of me being here. I'm sure by the end of the day there'll be pictures of us up on some website. I wish they'd allow my daughter her privacy, but people aren't that kind.

"JJ!" I hear my name called. I look over and see Austin Jones and his wife, Reese. They are here with their daughter. He plays for the hockey team and his wife is a famous singer.

"Hey, man, good to see you," I greet him as he stops next to me.

"You too. How's fatherhood treating you?" he asks, offering his hand to shake. We have met a few times over the years. I would not say he is one of my close friends, but he's a good guy, from what I know.

"It's going. Not something I ever thought I'd be doing right now, but I also wouldn't change it for anything," I tell him honestly. "How's your little one?" I ask, nodding over to where Reese and their daughter are playing.

"She's great, saying a few words now, almost walking. Reese thinks she'll be walking before her birthday in a few weeks."

"That's awesome. Evie said 'dada' for the first time the other day, and it about brought me to my knees."

"I remember when Nicole did that, and I had the same reaction. What is it with these little girls wrapping us around their little fingers?" he muses.

"No tour for Reese this summer?" I ask. I know most of the hockey guys leave town for the summer months.

"Nope. She wanted to take some more time off. She's got a few shows spread out over the summer at fairs and festivals, but for the most part, she's still enjoying being a mom first. We just got back home yesterday from a few weeks gone. She played the big CMA fest in Nashville earlier this month, and then we went to spend time with her family in Georgia for the rest of the month. I've got a youth hockey camp I'm helping with next week, so we came back for that."

"Nice. Yeah, today is my one day off this week, so I'm just spending it with my girls," I tell him.

"So, I'm guessing that headline was bullshit, then?" he muses.

"Don't get me started." I shake my head in disgust.

"Glad to hear that it wasn't true. A good woman in your life isn't a bad thing," he says, and I notice he's looking directly at his wife.

"I'll agree one thousand percent with you on that," I tell him as I notice Riley taking Evie out of the swing. They walk over just as Reese walks over with their daughter.

"Hi, I'm Riley," she introduces herself to both Reese and Austin. If she recognizes Reese, she does a damn good job hiding the fact.

"I'm Reese, and this is Austin and Nicole," Reese introduces all of them before I can.

"It's nice to meet you," Riley tells them.

"I know Austin because he plays for the Eagles," I interject, giving her some context as to whom I'm talking to.

"Oh, nice. That is the hockey team, right?" she questions.

"Yeah, babe. That is the NHL team in town," I chuckle as I answer her.

"How old is your daughter?" Riley asks Reese.

"She will be one next month!"

"She is such a cutie," Riley replies.

"How old is your daughter?" Reese asks.

"Six months," I answer for Riley. I know it makes her a little uncomfortable when people assume that Evie is her daughter.

"Such a fun age!" Reese exclaims. "Now that we are back in town, we should exchange numbers and get together with the girls. I can always use some other moms to hang out with that have little girls."

"That would be awesome. I've got my sister-in-law here in the neighborhood and two nieces, as well," Riley tells her as she pulls her cell from her back pocket. The girls move away, exchanging numbers as they head off with the kids again.

"I guess they've hit it off," Austin chuckles as we watch them walk away.

"I'd say so." I cannot help but laugh right along with him. "I can't say that I've met someone that Riley didn't get along with. She is pretty go-with-the-flow, laid back. I think that is why it has been so easy for the two of us. That, and I know deep in my bones that I can trust her with my daughter's life."

"She sounds like a good one, then. Glad you found her."

"All thanks to Derek, well, and Evie. She's Derek's little sister, so that created some challenges, but after he got over the shock, he has been good with it. Doesn't like seeing or hearing about any PDA," I say, chuckling. "But in the grand scheme of things, he's been pretty chill about it. I knew it could have been a whole lot different. I was expecting him to kick my ass, and he might have if Riley hadn't been there to step between us and put him in his place."

"I could see how that might complicate things," he says as his attention flashes to Reese and Nicole as she lets out a cry. "I'll be right back," he says before he takes off to where they are at the end of a slide.

I watch as he helps console his daughter. She didn't like something about going down the slide, I'm guessing.

"Hey, you," I whisper into Riley's ear, pressing a chaste kiss against the skin just below. "Having fun?" I ask, wrapping my hands around her as I stand flush behind her. Her ass presses firmly against my crotch, causing my dick to stir in my shorts. Not what I need popping up while we're at a public park.

"Hey, yourself," she replies, turning her neck slightly, giving me more access. I have to remind myself once again that we're in public, and I can't be pervy like I can when we're in my enclosed backyard.

"Want to go lay out the blanket and let Evie play with some toys?" I suggest.

"Sure," she says, then bends down to pick her up from the baby area they have here at this park.

I take Evie from her arms, flying her through the air like an airplane as we make our way over to the stroller. Riley pulls the blanket from the basket and spreads it out on the ground in a shaded spot in the grass. I take it she's done this many times. She spreads out a few toys from the stroller, as well, and I set Evie down, and she army crawls herself over to one of them. It instantly goes into her mouth, just like everything else she gets her little chubby fingers on.

"So, I have to ask, are you just that good at hiding your shock when you meet people, or do you not recognize Reese?"

She flashes me a small coy smile before answering. "When I first walked up, I didn't realize who she was. She just looked like another mom at the park with her daughter. But once she told me her name, I thought, no way, but then once you told me that Austin played for the Eagles, I recalled reading that she married a hockey player. I asked her after we walked away, and she was cool about it."

"I just wasn't sure. I mean, I know you're used to having your brother, and now me, in your life, but Reese is on another level of celebrity status in my book."

"She does have all of you beat out, I'd agree," Riley teases me.

"So, what's the plan for later? Did you text your brother to see if we're getting together?"

"I did, he was going to get back to me. Maybe you should try texting him," she tells me.

I pull out my phone and shoot off a text of my own.

JJ: What's up, man? Are we getting together tonight?

The three dots pop up for a few seconds, before disappearing and then popping back up a few seconds after that. I toss my phone on the blanket until he replies.

"Done. Looks like he's got a lot to say." I laugh as the bubbles continue to pop on and off the screen until my screen goes black as it times out.

Riley rolls her eyes, then lies back on the blanket and stretches out. Her tank top rides up slightly, showing off a small sliver of skin just above her shorts. I ache to drop a kiss to that exposed skin but hold myself back since we're in public. That wouldn't be a good picture to show up online.

"Stop looking at me like you're going to eat me," Riley says, rolling her head to look at me.

"How'd you even know I was doing that when your eyes were closed?" I ask, my eyebrows raised to my hairline.

"I can feel when they're on me. It's like a brand on my skin," she tells me.

"I'll brand your skin." I flash a grin as I wink at her.

"Don't be crass," she chides, giving me a stern look. Well, as stern of a look as she can while biting back a smile.

"Da-da-da," Evie starts to babble from where she is lying on the blanket playing with her toys.

"Yes, baby girl." I turn my attention back to her. I grab one of the toys that are just out of her reach, moving it back next to her. She abandons the toy she has in her hands and picks up the one I just set down. "I was thinking," I say, grabbing Riley's attention.

"What's that?" she questions.

"With my parents arriving tomorrow, how about I take you out on a date tomorrow night. You can get all dressed up, and I'll wine and dine you all night. Leave my parents at the house with Evie, and we'll take the night off, just the two of us."

"Mhmm, that sounds like heaven," she agrees with me.

"Then I'll plan it. Be ready to go by five and pack an overnight bag. I'm going to have you all to myself all night."

"Well, okay then," she says, flashing me her trademark smile.

My phone finally lights up with a reply from Derek, so I swipe the screen to open the text.

Derek: Hey, I think we are just going to chill at home tonight. Jillian is tired and just wants a quiet night.

JJ: Sounds good, man, see you tomorrow at practice.

Derek: See ya then.

"We're on our own for tonight. Derek said that Jillian is tired and just wants to have a chill night."

"Sounds good," Riley says as she shifts on the blanket. She rests her head in my lap, and my fingers go immediately to her hair. I remove the elastic keeping it held in the messy bun she put it into when we laid down on the blanket. I love running my fingers through it, and I know she loves it because she's told me a few times. Says that it relaxes her. "Let's order sushi and have an at-home date night."

"Sounds perfect," I tell her as I run a fingertip over her face.

We stay like that, just relaxing and enjoying the summer day as a family until Evie starts to get fussy. Riley changes her diaper quickly before we pick everything up and head back home for some lunch.

TWENTY

RILEY

"Mrs. Johnson, nice to see you again," I greet Justin's mom as she enters the house from the garage. I stayed home with Evie while he went to pick them up since she was still asleep when he had to go.

"Please, Riley, call me Julie," she says, wrapping me in a hug.

"All right," I wheeze out as she squeezes me hard.

"Sorry about that," she says sheepishly as she releases me. "Now, where is my granddaughter?" she asks as she just about bounces out of her sandals.

"She's playing in the jumper," I say, pointing into the kitchen. "I was just cleaning up from breakfast," I tell her as she takes off for the kitchen.

"Oh my!" she exclaims. "She's gotten so big! Evie girl, what have they been feeding you?" she asks her as I watch her lift her from the toy.

"She sure is growing like crazy. I just had to rotate her clothes to the twelve-month size already. Girlfriend loves her food," I tell Julie. I hear the door open again and look back to see Justin and his dad, Paul, come through it, a suitcase in each hand.

"I might have brought a few things for her." Julie looks at me, sheepishly.

"A few?" Paul questions, raising his brows at his wife. "Practically the entire baby store," he muses.

"Nice to see you again, Paul," I greet him as he sets the suitcases down and goes to his wife's side to say hello to his granddaughter. His face lights up as he smiles down at her, dropping a kiss to the top of her head. This little girl has so many people who love her unconditionally. I can only hope that it makes up for the fact that her mother isn't in her life.

"Good to see you again, Riley. How's my son treating you?" he asks as Justin slides up next to me. He places his arm around me possessively then kisses the top of my head.

"Just fine," I tell him honestly.

"That's good. Believe it or not, we did raise him with manners," Paul chuckles.

"Is that so?" I say as if I do not believe his statement.

"Yep, a Boy Scout, as well," Julie tells me.

"Okay, okay. I am right here, guys. Can you at least wait to talk shit about me until I'm gone at practice?" he protests.

"Of course. I brought your baby books along to share with Riley, so on you go. I'll tell her all your embarrassing stories while you're gone throwing a ball around," his mom says, just as sweetly as pie, as she flashes her son a shit-eating grin.

"Mom," Justin groans. "Please don't scare Riley off."

"Never. If she can put up with your shenanigans, then

she's a keeper in my book," his mom tells him matter-of-factly.

Paul steps away and takes their suitcases down to the guest room while I follow Julie outside with Evie. Justin had to get ready and head off to practice for the next few hours. We will see him again later this afternoon, and then, of course, he is whisking me away for our date. Kind of hard to believe that this will be our first actual date with just the two of us. We always have Evie with us, which I do not mind one bit, but it will be nice to just be the two of us. Not have to worry about feeding her or bedtime or being loud or interrupted by a crying baby.

Once outside, Julie sits down on the grass with Evie, a few toys scattered around the two of them. "I want you to know how thankful we are that you came into Justin's life when you did. We were so worried about him when he first called us to tell us about Evie, but after that first trip out, it calmed some of those fears, and now seeing the three of you together, you guys make the perfect little family. I hope he expresses his gratitude and makes you feel that way."

"Thank you," I tell her, not really knowing where to take this conversation. "I love both of them," I say, being as honest as I can. "I still clam up a little bit when people just assume that she's my daughter, but I get it. She looks like she could be, based on her skin tone and hair color," I tell her as she looks down at Evie. "I usually just avoid answering people by not correcting the assumption. Figure it is not really any of their business that I am her nanny, but also her dad's girlfriend. It *is* kind of weird territory."

"It is, but y'all will figure out what works for you. Who

cares what people think or assume? If the three of you are happy and healthy, that is all that matters in the end. And I would say this little girl is pretty dang lucky to have you in her life as a strong female role model. If one day you truly step into the role of her mother, or just stay as a friend, she's lucky to have you."

Tears prick my eyes at Julie's kind words. "Thank you," I say, just above a whisper. "I can only hope Justin and Evie feel the same way."

"Don't you worry, honey. My boy is head over heels in love with you. I have never seen him like this in his entire twenty-eight years."

"That's good," I muse.

"Now, why don't you go start getting ready for tonight, take the day and go get a manicure and pedicure, pamper yourself for your special night out. I hear that son of mine is whisking you away for the night, and this little love bug gets to have a night with Grandma and Grandpa."

"She does," I agree, smiling at the two of them. Evie is playing along happily with Julie right by her. "You're sure?" I ask as I look down at my toes that could really use a fresh coat of paint, and so could my chipped fingernails.

"Positive, and if I know my son as well as I think I do, he'd think the same thing."

"Okay, but promise me you'll call or text if anything goes wrong."

"I can promise, but I can also tell you that you've got nothing to worry about. I did raise that boy that you're so fond of, and he's still alive," she jokes.

"Of course," I agree, shaking my head at myself.

"Off you go," she says, shooing me away.

I have not had a day to pamper myself in a long time and I almost don't know what to do with myself. I slip my cell from my pocket to text Jillian to see if she wants to join me.

Riley: Want to join me for a pedicure? I've been kicked out by Justin's parents.

Jillian: Let me see if the neighbor girl is home and can watch the girls! If she is, then absolutely! That sounds like heaven right about now.

Riley: Sounds good.

The thought to invite Reese also pops into my head, and before I can talk myself out of it, I shoot her a text, as well.

Riley: Hey! I'm heading out last minute to get a pedicure, would you like to come with me? My SIL might also join.

Reese: OMG! Yes! I need some pamper time. When are you going, and to what place?

Riley: Ummm... good question! I haven't been to any of the places since moving here. Do you recommend a place close by that can take walk-ins? And I'm ready to go whenever.

Jillian: Cora will be here in about 10 minutes to watch the girls! So, I'll be ready after that. Do you want to swing by and pick me up?

Riley: Perfect! I also invited Reese Blackwood; do you know who she is? I met her at the park yesterday. Justin was talking to her husband, Austin.

Jillian: She's a sweetheart! You will love her! We've met at a few charity events the guys have all gone to, and I've run into her out and about in the neighborhood.

Riley: I asked if she recommended a salon nearby that takes walk-ins as I realized that I haven't been to any since moving here.

Reese: There's a place just outside of the neighborhood that takes walk-ins that I've been to a handful of times. Want to try them first? We can always go elsewhere if they can't get us in.

Riley: Sounds perfect! I've got to swing by and pick up my SIL, and we'll meet you there!

Reese: See you soon!

Riley: I'm on my way! Reese recommended the

place just outside the neighborhood; I said we'd just meet her there.

Jillian: Sounds good to me, that's where I go. See you when you get here.

I slip my flip flops on, grab my phone, wallet, and keys and head out the door. Less than five minutes later, I'm pulling in to pick up Jillian, who's already outside waiting on me.

"Sorry, I figured if you came inside, the girls would want to hold us up leaving," she says, getting in the car before I can get out.

"That's okay," I tell her before backing out.

"How's your day going?" she asks as I make our way out of the subdivision. I catch her up on Justin's parents arriving and how he is whisking me away for the night for a date night, how this outing was his mom's idea and all about our conversation before I left.

"His parents are great; I've met them a few times," she tells me as we pull up to the nail salon.

Reese is already inside, her feet in a tub of hot water. "Hey, girls!" she calls out once we are inside. "Grab your color and take a seat," she says, motioning to the chairs next to her that are being filled with water.

"Hi, Reese," Jillian greets her, "good to see you again."

"This is your sister-in-law?" she asks me with excitement filling her voice.

"The one and only," I confirm.

"So, your brother is Derek?"

"You are correct again," I tell her.

"It's all making so much sense now," she says. "I think we're all going to be good friends," she states matter-of-factly as Jillian and I both select our colors and sit in the big massage chairs. I relax as my feet slide into the hot water, and the massage rollers start working up and down my back.

"Oh my god, this was just what I needed," I moan a moment later.

"You and me both. I might need to make this a regular thing. Especially the farther along in this pregnancy I get," Jillian says. I look over, and she's got her eyes closed as the chair massages away at her back.

"Amen to that, sister. I came all the time when I was pregnant with Nicole," Reese tells us.

"Do you know where JJ is taking you tonight?" Jillian asks once the techs start on our toes a few minutes later.

"He's told me nothing except to be ready by five and to pack an overnight bag."

"Ooh, sounds like he's got some sexy times planned," Reese teases me.

"I'm sure he does," Jillian says, bouncing her eyebrows at me.

"You guys are almost as bad as he is," I joke right along with them. "I'm guessing a hotel and dinner are involved, as well," I tell them, "but without knowing where we're going to dinner, I'm a little stumped with what I should wear tonight."

"You need something sexy, make him sweat it out during dinner," Reese suggests. "I know the perfect store, not far away, that we could go to after here and get you a cute little number for tonight."

"I like that idea!" Jillian adds. "We could also grab some lunch on our way."

"Is baby boy hungry?" I ask her, and she just shrugs her shoulders at me like, what do you expect, I've got a bowling ball in my stomach.

"Sounds like we've got more plans today!" I state, knowing it's easier to just go along with them than to try and go against whatever it is that they are scheming up. "That won't be a problem with the sitter, will it?" I ask Jillian.

"Nope, she said she was free all day. I'll just send her a text that we're going to grab some lunch and then stop at the store before coming back."

"Okay," I reply.

"And I'll text my husband that he's on Daddy duty for a few hours."

"How's he handling that?" Jillian asks Reese.

"Like a pro. He was so cute when she was first born with how nervous he was to hold her, but after a day or two he got over the fears and is just smitten with her. She's definitely a Daddy's girl."

"Derek was the same way when Addison was born. When Penny came along, he was right in there as soon as she was born, taking over. It will be interesting to see how he is with a boy this time around."

"I'm sure he'll be just fine, and he's going to be teaching that boy to pitch a baseball before he can even walk, you just watch," I interject.

"Probably," she agrees, knowing Derek as well as we both do.

"Do you think Austin will try and get Nicole to play hockey?" I ask Reese.

"Oh, he's already counting down the months until he can go buy her first pair of skates. I think the moment will be more special for him than it will be for Nicole," she says, chuckling.

"Are you working on any new music?" Jillian asks Reese.

"Yep, I have been writing like crazy with a handful of writers, along with my favorite two back in Nashville, Stacey and Lee. They have become a little popular in the last few years, but always make time for me, which I am so grateful for! The plan right now is to head back into the studio in the fall and start recording for a spring record release. Then I'll head out on a full tour next year. I'll have to probably kick it off before Austin is done with the season, so we'll have to juggle that, but then he'll just join us wherever we are once he's done for the season. The same will go when he's due back in the fall for camp and the start of the new season."

"Do you have a nanny that travels with you, then?" I ask, not sure how that works.

"Probably. I have not gone on a full tour yet since Nicole was born, so Austin or my mom has just come along with me to take care of Nicole while I'm on stage. Once all the tour dates are set, and we know how much of them he cannot be with me, we will make that call. I would prefer to just have family since the bus quarters are tight, but I also feel bad asking my mom to come out on the road with me for weeks or months at a time. It can be hard to go from city to city, night after night. Eating catered food most days and sleeping weird hours while rolling down the road."

"Makes sense." I nod my head as I digest everything that she must have to consider now that she's got a baby. "I never even considered everything that went into touring, especially with a baby and family."

"It's going to be different, that is for sure," she agrees. "Even just going out for one or two show weekends this summer has been so different, and I've had Austin or my mom with me for all of them. Being on a bus with an almost walking toddler is not an easy feat, I can't imagine what it will be like when she is walking."

Our conversation flows over the hour as we finish up our pedicures. I picked out a bright pink, Jillian, a bright orange, and Reese, a bright red. With our toes all pretty and my fingernails also painted for tonight, we head out, first for some lunch and then to the store to find me the perfect outfit for tonight.

TWENTY-ONE
JUSTIN

"Listen up," Coach Roberts calls out as he enters the locker room from the dugout. We retreat into the locker room rather than stay out on the field because of how hot it is after a long practice. The air feels good on my warm skin. I suck down a bottle of ice-cold water as he looks around, waiting to get everyone's attention. "Jose is out on IR for an unknown amount of time. He is going to require surgery and rehab after that. We've called up Lucas Black, so please welcome him to the team," he tells the room at large. Jose is one of our best outfielders and had a nasty collision during a game last week and screwed up his shoulder.

They have never called this kid up, so I don't know much about him, but my initial instinct just looking at him is he's a punk kid with a chip on his shoulder. He does not look a day over twenty-one, so he is probably young and cocky. Maybe he is the answer to my problem with the press.

"Welcome," a few of the guys call out to him, and he gives out a few head nods around the room. Yep, he's a cocky fucker. *I think I'll like him*, I say to myself. With Coach done talking to everyone, I pull my drenched clothes off and head for the showers. Knowing that I've got a date ahead of me tonight has me ready to blow out of this place as soon as possible.

I take the world's quickest shower, pack my shit, and am out of the door before most guys are even dried off and dressed. "Where're you off to in such a hurry?" Derek calls to my back.

"Got a hot date with your sister," I call out over my shoulder.

"You better treat her right, or I'll kick your ass tomorrow!" he calls back to me.

"Like her prince fuckin charming!" I tell him before the door to the locker room closes. I laugh my way to my car, pop the locks, and toss my bag into the back seat. I roll the windows down and open the sunroof, enjoying the sunny day and wind as I drive home.

"Hello!" I call out once I'm home. The house is quiet and dark, so I go in search of everyone. I find my parents outside with Evie, in the pool. "I'm home," I call out, opening the door. "Where's Riley?" I ask, looking around for her.

"We sent her off to go pamper herself today before your date tonight," Mom tells me as she floats around the pool.

"Good thinking, I wish I'd thought of that."

"I told her just the same," Mom tells me.

"Has she been gone long?" I ask, looking at my watch and seeing that it's only three o'clock.

"Yep, she left mid-morning. Texted awhile ago that she is out with Jillian and Reese. They were going to get some lunch and then go shopping. Something about the girls insisting that she have a new outfit for tonight and wouldn't take no for an answer."

"Okay, I'll just text her to see when she'll be back."

JJ: Just got home, will you be here soon?

Riley: Maybe 30 minutes? We still need to check out, but Jillian is trying a few things on still.

JJ: No rush; have a good time.

Riley: It's been a fun day! I just love Reese.

JJ: Glad to hear it. See you when you get home. I can't wait to see what you've picked out for tonight. Hopefully, it is something skimpy. :winky face:

Riley: You will just have to wait and see... :kissy face:

"Sounds like they're having a good time and will be home within the hour or so."

"I figured she could use a girls' day out of the house and

without the responsibility of Evie," Mom tells me as I take a seat on one of the deck chairs.

"I'm going to go pack my bag for tonight, you guys okay out here? Need anything?"

"I'd take a beer if you have one in the fridge," my dad says from the chair next to me.

"Should have some, I'll go grab you one. Want anything, Mom?"

"Nope, I'm good for now."

I stand up and head inside. I grab a beer quick for my dad and take it back out to him then head in and pull out a change of clothes, along with my toiletries kit. With the amount of travel I do, I've always got it packed and ready to go. I top off a few of the bottles and toss it into my bag. I don't need much since we'll be back sometime tomorrow morning before I have to head to the field before our afternoon game.

I finished packing and head out to the kitchen, grabbing a Gatorade from the fridge just as I hear the garage door open. I look around the corner and see Riley coming in, a few bags hanging from each of her hands. "Hey, babe, did you buy out the entire store?" I tease her.

"Felt like it, but Jillian and Reese insisted I get it all."

"Do I get a personal fashion show?" I ask, raising my brows in a suggestive question.

"Not until later," she tells me. "Now go away while I unpack all of this, pack my bag and get dressed for tonight. And no peeking," she scolds me. I stalk over to her, wrapping my arms around her as I lift her off the ground. I crash my lips to hers in a possessive kiss.

"Maybe we should stop at the hotel before dinner," I say against her lips.

"Not happening," she insists. "You'll ruin my hair and makeup if we do that, and the next hour of me getting ready will be pointless."

"If you insist. But after? You. Are. Mine," I tell her, nipping at her jaw between each word. "I hope you're not expecting to get much sleep tonight," I warn as I set her back on her feet and smack her ass as she turns to head to the bedroom.

It feels like forever before Riley comes out of the room, but really it's only just over an hour. I have to swallow my damn tongue when I see her. She's pulled her hair up into a half-twisty half-down style. Minimal makeup highlights her eyes and lips, and my mind jumps directly into the gutter with that color staining them. My eyes track down her body. She's got a one-piece, off the shoulder outfit that hits her mid-thigh. I have no idea what they call this style of outfit, but it looks like it was made for her. My eyes trail down her legs and find her feet in simple, yet elegant sandals that wrap around her ankles.

I hear a whistle from behind me and turn to find my dad whistling at Riley. "Damn, son, you're one lucky man tonight," he says, and I catch the blush as it stains Riley's cheeks at his appraisal.

"You're already married, old man, so paws off my woman," I tease my dad.

"You already made me a grandpa once this year, maybe hold off on doing it again tonight," he quips right back at me. That is all it takes for me to think of just that. What it would be like to experience a pregnancy with Riley. I missed so much with not knowing that Erica was even pregnant that I hope I get to experience it one day with Riley, whenever that might be.

"No promises," I give it right back to him.

"Would you two behave?" Mom asks, smacking Dad on the chest as she moves to stand next to him. Evie is in her arms, and as soon as she's next to Dad, he takes Evie from Mom, much to her dismay. "You look stunning tonight, Riley," Mom compliments her.

"Thank you," she shyly accepts the compliments. "My sister-in-law insisted this was the perfect outfit for tonight. It would work if we went somewhere fancy or somewhere more casual. And it's super comfortable to boot, so it was a win-win," she tells us as I close the distance between us. I pull her into my arms, burying my face in the crook of her neck. I breathe in deep, getting a lungful of her shampoo and perfume mixture.

"Ready?" I ask, standing back slightly. I can't help it and have to drop a quick kiss to her lips.

"Yep, just got to grab my bag and say goodbye to Evie," she tells me, and my heart about melts that she doesn't want to leave without saying goodbye to my daughter.

⁓

WE FINALLY MAKE IT OUT OF THE HOUSE, THIRTY-PLUS minutes later. I head straight for the restaurant I made reservations at. I requested a patio table, seeing as the weather is perfect for it. The Capital Grille is a popular steakhouse in downtown Indianapolis, one that I was lucky to score a reservation at. Sometimes flexing my name recognition helps just a little bit in my favor.

We're seated quickly, a bottle of champagne already waiting beside the table in a bucket of ice.

"Good evening," a waiter says, approaching the side of the table moments after we are seated. "I'm Jeffery, and I'll be taking care of you tonight. Can I start you out with a glass of champagne or something else from the bar?" he asks, holding out the bottle for us to inspect.

"Babe?" I leave the decision up to Riley on what she wants to drink.

"You can't ever go wrong with fancy champagne," she says, motioning to the bottle. Jeffery untwists the top and pops the cork like he's done it a time or ten.

"Would you like for me to go over tonight's specials, or did you want to take a minute to look over the menu?" he asks as he expertly pours us each a glass of the bubbly liquid.

"Are they just what's listed here?" Riley asks him, holding up the single sheet menu page we were given when seated.

"Yes, ma'am," he tells her.

"I'm good then, thank you," she tells him.

"And you, sir?" he asks, turning his attention to me after replacing the champagne in the ice bucket.

"I'm good, but can we get two shrimp cocktails to start out with, please?"

"Of course, I'll get that in right away," he says before stepping away from the table. I reach across the small table and grab Riley's hand in mine as we both read over everything on the menu.

"What are you thinking?" I ask once I've had the chance to look it all over.

"I'm leaning towards the eight-ounce filet with a side of lobster mac and cheese. I'm sure that will be more than I can eat, but it all sounds so good."

"Order one of everything for all I care," I tell her.

"I'd be as big as a house if I did that." She laughs, and I feel it down to my toes.

"Did you have fun today?" I ask after Jeffery returns with our appetizer and takes our dinner order.

"I did. It was the best-unexpected girls' day that I didn't realize I needed. We talked and laughed basically all day. My cheeks hurt from smiling so much while I was with Reese and Jillian. It was also fascinating, learning all about Reese and being a singer and about life on the road."

"I can only imagine how hard that is, especially now that they have a kid."

"Yep, she wasn't sure exactly what that was going to look like once she goes on a big tour."

"Lots for them to figure out before then. Did she say when that is? Austin said that she didn't have one planned for this year."

"She said probably next spring it would start, and go well into the fall."

We fall into a comfortable conversation, a lot about Evie, but also a lot about the months to come. The food comes quickly, and we stuff our faces with a delicious meal.

"Can I tempt the two of you with dessert this evening?" Jeffery asks as he clears our plates away.

"I don't think I can take one more bite of anything," Riley tells him, and I agree.

"No problem, let me get this cleared away and I'll bring the check," he politely tells us.

"So, where are we off to after this?" she asks once it is just the two of us again.

"Well, I thought we could drive the few blocks over and walk around the Central Canal. There are usually artists out, and it's lit up at night, so it's a beautiful walk along the canal. Then I'm taking you back to the hotel where I have lots of naked plans for you tonight."

"I'd be okay with skipping the walk and going right to the hotel..." she says, trailing off as Jeffery reappears at the edge of the table. I pull my credit card out faster than it takes for him to place the bill folder on the table. We need out of here and now. He whisks the card and bill away, returning only a moment later with the receipt for me to sign. I scroll my signature, along with a hefty tip for his excellent service on the bottom, before I practically drag Riley out of the restaurant.

"Do you know what you do to me?" I ask once we are back at my car. I pin Riley against the side of the car, dropping my lips to hers before she can answer me. Her hands sink into my shirt. I press against her a little harder, letting her feel just how hard I am. Letting her know just what she's doing to me tonight.

"Take me to the hotel, Justin," she whispers in my ear before sucking the lobe between her teeth—I about cum in my pants at that. I rapidly open her door, helping her in before I shut the door and round the front of the car as quickly as I can. Thank fuck the hotel isn't that far away. Traffic is also on my side, and we swiftly make it.

After a quick stop at the front desk to check-in, we are in the elevator and on our way up to the suite level. With it just being one night, I didn't think we needed the penthouse, although having that full private top deck would have been something. I could think of a few activities that we could have partaken in out on it, but that will have to wait until another time.

"You're not tired, are you?" I ask as Riley rests her head against my shoulder on our ride up.

"Nope, I'm ready for whatever you have planned."

"You sure you want to commit to *anything?*" I ask, raising my eyebrows in question.

"Bring it," she fires right back at me as she moves to stand in front of me, so we are now facing each other. Our arms automatically wrap around one another.

"What if I wanted to tie you up and tease you all night?" I ask, just testing the waters, here. I notice her eyes dilate, and I know that she's thought of a little bondage at some point.

"I'd be open to it," she whispers, obviously a little nervous about the idea.

"Not happening tonight, but I won't rule it out in the future." I've never been into that scene, but hell, I'll give almost anything a try at least once.

We finally make it to our room, and as soon as the door clicks shut, I drop our two overnight bags on the floor and scoop Riley up in my arms, carrying her over to the bed and depositing her in the center.

"Not so fast, mister," she stops me, pushing against my chest.

I stand up quickly, never wanting her to think I would not stop when she asks. "Everything okay?" I ask.

"Yes, I just have a little surprise of my own for you, and I need to use the bathroom first," she tells me as she slides off the bed and trails off to the bathroom, grabbing her bag along the way. I blow out a breath then walk over to the large windows overlooking the city while I wait for her to emerge from the bathroom.

As soon as I hear the click of the door opening, I turn around and about fall to my knees. Riley is standing in the doorway, covered in a few scraps of delicate lingerie. I waste no time closing the distance between the two of us. I want nothing more than to unwrap her like the present she is. "You are incredible," I tell her, pulling her into my arms. I can't not touch her when we're this close to one another.

I slide my hands over her mostly exposed skin, taking my time to memorize the way she feels in this moment. Once my hands reach her bare ass cheeks, I lift her up until she wraps her legs around my waist. I take her back over to the bed, depositing her once again in the center. This time when I box her in, she looks up at me with nothing but lust in her eyes.

"I'm having so many thoughts right now," I tell her as my lips find bare skin just above the swell of her breasts. I show no mercy, sucking her nipples through the lace of her bra cups.

"Justin!" She gasps my name as I grind my dick against her pussy. The friction the lace is providing is driving her crazy, I'm sure. That, coupled with not giving her direct contact where she wants it most, but we'll get to that. We've got all night to lose ourselves in one another.

Evie might have turned my world upside down in a matter of minutes when Erica dropped her on my doorstep, but it was Riley that threw the curve ball I never saw coming, but I'm damn sure glad she did.

EPILOGUE
RILEY

December

"Morning, pretty girl." I flip on the light in Evie's room and find her standing up in her crib. She's gotten so big these past few months, and I can't believe that she'll be one in just a few more weeks.

"How're my favorite girls this morning?" Justin asks as I walk into our room where he's still lounging in bed. We've been enjoying our lazy mornings now that he's in the offseason. The Lightning made it into the playoffs but just missed on making it to the World Series. I snuggle up to him, Evie between the two of us. She crawls from my arms and onto his lap, laying her head against his chest.

"I think we're pretty good," I tell him as I sit here watching them together. Nothing melts my heart faster than observing him as a dad. He's so good with her, and you'd never guess he didn't always want this life.

"Dada," Evie chatters, pointing at Justin's face.

"Yes, baby?" he asks her, pretending to chew on her fingers and making her fall into a fit of giggles.

"Mama?" she says, pointing at me. I gasp in shock, and Justin's eyes fly to mine.

"What did you say, Evie?" he asks her.

"Mama," she says, clear as day a second time.

We've never really talked about this yet. We've never referred to me as her mom, always Ry or Riley. Justin's eyes burn into mine, looking for clarification from *me*. I have no idea what to do. I don't ever want to confuse her, but I'd be honored for her to think of me as her mother figure.

"Mama, I kinda like the sound of that," Justin finally says.

Tears. Tears spring to my eyes and roll down my face—the pure happiness in this little moment. One so private, so pure, so us. Just the three of us, together in bed and adding another first together. "Are you sure?" I ask through my tears.

"There is no one else I'd rather Evie look to as her mother. You've been here for her since she arrived on my doorstep. You've kissed every boo-boo, picked out almost every cute outfit she's worn, pushed her countless times on the swing at the park, floated around with her for endless hours in the pool. So, to answer your question, yes. I'm sure that I want my daughter to look to you as her mother. A strong, confident, beautiful woman, who dropped everything in her life to make our lives as normal as can be. We love you so much and are so grateful for every sacrifice you've made for us. You could have easily thrown in the towel when things got tough, but you didn't. You showed your strength and love for us by sticking it out during those times. Evie might not realize it now, but the way you showed complete grace when your name was dragged through the headlines, and people yelled at you and called you names at games, would show her how to be the strong woman I hope she one day grows to be. And there's no one better than you to show her that path."

The tears fall faster down my cheeks at Justin's words. He pulls me closer to him, kissing my tear-soaked lips. "I love you," I whisper against them before I'm pushed back by a squirming Evie. "I love you, too, baby girl," I tell her as my tears turn to laughter.

"Evie and I have a question for you," Justin says, pulling my attention back to his.

"Yes, I'll make pancakes and bacon for breakfast," I tease him, knowing exactly what he's going to ask.

"That's good to know, but that wasn't what we were wondering," he says, flashing a smug smile.

Justin leans over the bed and comes up with a small gift bag. I'm so confused by a few things. First, where in the heck was he hiding a gift bag, and for how long? Secondly, why does he have a present for me? Christmas is just a couple of weeks away, and it isn't my birthday. "Here, open this," he says as he sets the bag in front of me. Evie tries to lean forward and grab the tissue paper that is poking out the top, but I swoop it out of her reach just in time.

I reach into the bag and pull out a onesie, unfolding it to read the front. My eyes go wide as I take in what it says.

"Will you marry my daddy?"

My eyes snap to Justin, who is now holding an open

ring box and attempting to keep Evie from grabbing it from him as she crawls all over him.

"We love you and want you to be part of our family officially. Will you marry me and become Evie's mom for real?" Justin asks me, a huge smile covering his lips.

"Oh my," I gasp, covering my mouth with my hand. "Yes!" I cry out, and he pulls me back into his arms, kissing me deeply as Evie smacks us in the face with her little chubby hands.

"We've got her forever," Justin says to Evie as he shifts her to sit up higher on the bed between our pillows. He finally slips the ring out of the box and onto my finger.

"So, does this mean I can't refer to myself as the nanny anymore?" I tease him, looking down at the enormous ring he just placed on my finger.

"I think fiancée has a better ring to it." He winks at me. "And once I put your name on my bank account, do I really need to keep paying you?" He smirks.

"I've already told you that you could stop paying me," I say as I plant another kiss to his lips.

"I know, but you wouldn't let me put your name on my bank account, so will you now?"

"It kind of scares me to think of my name on an account with so many digits in it."

"Why?"

"Because that's a lot of freaking money. You know most people could only dream of making as much money as you do, right?"

"I'm aware." He smirks—*the jerk*. "But I also know that I'm going to take care of my family for the rest of my life.

Make my wife happy, maybe have a few more kids," he tells me, and my eyebrows raise in question.

"A few, huh?"

"I missed that whole part of parenthood the first time around, and I know how much Evie has changed my life for the good, that I want that again. I want that with you. I want to see what Evie is like as a big sister, and, god willing, what she's like as a teenager. I want it all, and I want it with you."

"You sure are a charmer this morning," I tease him. "You sure you're feeling okay?"

"I'm feeling on top of the world. The best woman in the world just said yes when I asked if she'd marry me and become my daughter's mom."

"Okay, way to make a girl cry again." I wipe at my eyes because tears spring to them once again this morning.

"How about we go make those pancakes and bacon?" he asks, changing the subject. "You ready for some breakfast, Evie girl?" he asks her, picking her up and blowing a raspberry on her belly. "Let's go, fiancée," he says, smacking my ass just before he rolls off the bed. I watch as he walks out of the room, his daughter on his hip, and hear her call out, "mama" just as they clear the doorway.

Hearing her call me that takes my breath away again. I grab my cell from the nightstand where I've still got it plugged in. I snap a picture of my hand, displaying the massive rock on my finger, and text an image to Jillian and Reese in our group text.

Riley: So... this just happened!!! {Picture of the ring on my finger}

Jillian: OMG, CONGRATULATIONS!!!!! (And PS, about damn time he asked. He talked to your dad and Derek over Thanksgiving, and I've had the hardest time holding that information in.)

Reese: YES!!!! I'm so happy for you guys! <3

Riley: HE WHAT? And thanks! <3 I'm still in shock.

Riley: Also, I have to tell someone, and I know you will both love this. Evie called me Mama this morning. Not once, twice, but THREE times! <3 That girl has my heart in her little chubby hands.

Jillian: Awww, engagements, Mama. Dang, not much will top today for you.

Reese: Awww, that's the best**!**

Reese: This calls for a girls' night soon. When will you be ready to leave that little man with Daddy and go out for some mommy time, Jillian?

Jillian: Maybe soon? Let's get over the holiday hump, and we'll talk about it.

Reese: As long as it's before I have to leave for my

press tour and then straight into rehearsals for said tour.

Jillian: I promise to make time for you ladies before that.

Riley: We've always got Evie's birthday party in January we can get together at!

Recse: That's fine and all, but we need some kid-free, mommy time to celebrate you! I'm talking dinner, drinks ~ the whole works.

Riley: If you insist. :winky face: I'll let you twist my arm and take me out.

Riley: Okay, gotta go. My people are calling for me to make them breakfast.

Jillian: Tell that fiancé of yours to make you some breakfast.

I pop into the bathroom quickly, running a brush through my bed head then pulling it up into a messy bun. I can't believe that Justin proposed, in bed, while we both were in our PJs, bed head and all. Even with all of that, I still wouldn't change it for anything. I wouldn't trade it for the perfectly planned dinner out, public event, or anything else. We've done our damnedest to keep our relationship as private as possible, and I wouldn't want this to be any different.

I join my little family in the kitchen. I find Evie already in her highchair, munching away on some dry cereal and drinking milk from her bottle. "You didn't want to try the sippy cup?" I ask Justin as I start to pull out the ingredients for pancakes. I make them so often I don't even need to look at the recipe anymore.

"Not really. She constantly throws it on the floor when I give it to her."

I laugh at him. "You know she only does that for you. She knows that you'll pick it up a thousand times."

"I still don't know how you've taught her that." He looks at me like I've solved the world's greatest mysteries.

"I guess it's magic," I tell him, shrugging my shoulders.

"So, when are we going to tell people?" he asks.

"I already texted Jillian and Reese," I tell him.

"Good, what did they say?" he asks, leaning against the counter with his back against it so that he's facing me.

"They were both super excited and happy for us. Jillian was happy that you finally asked. Said that she'd had the hardest time keeping it from me. She let me in on the little fact that you talked to Dad and Derek about it over Thanksgiving," I tell him, looking at him a little accusingly.

"Had to ask for permission," he says, giving me a pointed look.

"I guess you did well. Was this morning how you planned to ask?" I question him.

"Nope, that was spontaneous. With Evie calling you Mama, I knew it was time, so I just went with it."

"Where in the heck were you hiding that present, then, and for how long?"

"I just put it under the bed yesterday when it arrived in the mail. I was trying to decide between asking you sometime around Christmas or New Years. I was going to have Evie wear the shirt, but this morning worked out just as perfectly."

"I'd have to agree with that," I tell him, leaning over to kiss him. I break away from his lips to keep from letting the kiss get too heated. I pour batter on the grill, listening to the satisfying sizzle it makes when the batter hits the hot surface.

"That smells good, anything I can help with?" Justin asks, dropping a kiss to my cheek.

"I've got this under control. You just sit there and look good," I tell him.

Justin

"The Indianapolis Lightning's Justin "JJ" Johnson was once known as the player of the team. When a daughter was dropped on his doorstep last spring, JJ made an abrupt one-hundred-and-eighty-degree change, becoming a family man, one that is about to marry the woman he refers to as the love of his life. He sat down with one of our reporters for an exclusive

interview."

I READ OVER THE HEADLINE AND SUBSEQUENT ARTICLE that will be released tomorrow. This time, I was involved from start to finish and know what this article will say, and I know exactly what images they'll be printing, all of them approved by Riley and me.

"Justin, tell me what your favorite thing about being a dad is?"

I can remember back just a few short weeks to when I sat down for this interview; the memories come flooding back to me as I read over my quotes. *"Oh, wow. There's so much that has happened in the last ten months. Sometimes it is hard to believe that it's been ten months since Evie came into my life, but yet, at the same time, it feels like it was just yesterday. I have to say, the best part is just watching her grow. Watching her experience things for the first time. The first time she called my fiancée, Riley, Mama, both of their eyes lit up. It was an extraordinary moment for the three of us. Riley has been the only mother figure that she's known, and that wasn't something that we made light of, but it was also the moment that I knew it was time to propose, so I did. Right there in bed, with my two girls, bed head, and morning breath. It was perfect."*

"Riley started as your nanny for Evie, is that correct?" the reporter asked.

"That's correct. Riley is also my best friend, Derek Smyth's, little sister. The night that Evie's mom brought her

to my house and then just left; the first person I called was Derek. I knew that he or his wife, Jillian, would know what to do with a baby, seeing as they had two kids of their own at the time. Not ten minutes later, Derek arrived, but with Riley, not Jillian. She swooped in and calmed my daughter down. She stayed the night and took care of her like she was her own. That morphed into me hiring her to be Evie's nanny. I obviously don't work a normal eight to five work schedule, so trying to hire someone was going to be challenging. Riley had just moved here to be near her family and hadn't found a job yet. She offered to watch Evie on a trial basis to make sure the arrangement worked for both of us. Long story short, I'd say it worked out just fine."

I remember answering that question, as well, smirking at my honest answer. Riley joined us shortly after that, answering a few questions on what it was like to be attacked verbally in the tabloids and by jealous female fans. It was a bit hard to listen to her retell what she went through. But as much as I hate that part of things, it's part of our story. It helped make us stronger, made us turn to each other more.

"Hey, baby?" I call out, putting my iPad down after I finish reading over the article. I'm one hundred percent happy with the outcome and hope she is, as well.

"Yeah?" she asks, peeking her head around the door.

"Did you read this yet?" I ask.

"Not yet, was it good?" she questions.

"Yeah, I really like it."

"Good, I'm glad. I was hoping that you would. We poured our hearts out to them, so I'm glad they got it right," she tells me as she walks over and sits down on my lap. I wrap my arms around her torso as hers go around my shoulders, one of her hands threading into my hair.

"So, I was thinking..." she says, trailing off.

"What's that?"

"What if we went and got married at the courthouse before you leave for spring training?"

"But what about the destination wedding? I thought you wanted something this fall?"

"I did, but," she says, reaching behind me to grab something I didn't even know was there. She hands me a little T-shirt and I hold it up so I can read it.

"*Big Sister in Training.*"

"Are, are you pregnant?" I ask, absolutely astonished.

She just nods her head yes, tears streaming down her cheeks. "I took a test yesterday morning, and it was positive. I took, like, five more just to make sure it wasn't a fluke, and they were all the same."

"Fuck, yes!" I growl, pulling her in tightly and burying my face in her neck. "I can't wait to watch you grow with this baby. Thank you, thank you, thank you! I love you so much, all three of you," I mumble into her neck before pulling back to lay one on her lips.

"So, I take that as a yes?" she asks a moment later.

"I'll marry you today if that'd make you happy," I tell her honestly.

"I don't know that we can do it that fast, but I thought before you have to report for camp in a few weeks."

"Then, consider it done," I tell her and mean every word.

Justin
Five days later

"To my wife!" I toast along with our small group of family and friends who we invited over for an intimate wedding reception at our house. "The best woman I know, the one I get to love and drive nuts every day for the rest of my life," I say, and everyone laughs, knowing that I'm probably not lying.

I pull her into my arms and then lead her out onto the makeshift dance floor for our first dance as husband and wife. While the song plays in the background, I hold her close. "I have one last surprise for you tonight," I tell her just as the song ends.

"What's that?" she asks, pulling back enough to look up at me. Pregnancy sure looks good on her, and she isn't even showing yet.

"It wouldn't be a surprise if I told you," I tease her. "But it is inside. I'll give it to you once everyone is gone."

"Your cock isn't a surprise; I already know I'll be riding it later," she boldly tells me, causing that appendage to stir in my slacks.

"That's not what I was referring to," I bark out. She's gotten bolder over the months, telling me precisely what she wants in the bedroom, and I'm all over that shit.

"It's something else. Something from Evie and me," I tell her.

"Well, now you have me curious. Can you just give it to me? The suspense is killing me." She starts to whine.

"I guess," I tell her as I lead her inside the house. I grab the Manila envelope from the counter and hand it over. "Open it," I tell her.

I watch as she slips her finger under the flap, opening it up and pulling the papers out. I watch as her eyes widen as she reads over the pages. I know exactly what they say, what they'll mean to her. The significance they'll have to Evie and to me, in a way.

"You want me to adopt her?" she asks, tears already pricking her eyes and sliding down her cheeks.

"I do. You're Evelyn's mom, Riley. Might as well make it official with the courts, and now that we're married, it will make the process even easier."

"Yes!" she cries. "Where do I sign?"

"Last page, where the tab is," I tell her as I watch as she flips to the last page and signs her name across the line. "I also got word from my attorney that Erica signed the paperwork terminating all of her parental rights, so we never have to worry about her coming back and trying to take Evie from us. It's just the three, well, four of us, from here on out."

"I'm stunned silent. I don't even know what to say," she says.

"You've already said everything I needed to hear," I tell her, pulling her into my arms and kissing her. I sink into her mouth, tasting the sweet hint from the sparkling cider that she drank during the toast instead of the champagne we served our guests.

"Do you know how long it will take for me to become her mom?" she asks once we break apart.

"The wait is over, you're already her mom in all the ways that matter most."

THE INDIANAPOLIS LIGHTNING ARE BACK WITH LUCAS Black, finding his way to a happily ever after with the one woman he can't help but drive crazy! The Screw Ball is available on your favorite retailer!

COMING SOON

Ryker
San Francisco Shockwaves Book 1
May 19, 2022
Pre-Order on your favorite retailer!
Add on Goodreads today!

***

Nothing Bundt Forever
Sweet Valley, Tennessee Book 2
July 27, 2022
Pre-order on your favorite retailer!
Add on Goodreads today!

***

Aiden

San Francisco Shockwaves Book 2
October 20, 2022
Pre-Order on your favorite retailer today!
Add on Goodreads today!

ALSO BY SAMANTHA LIND

INDIANAPOLIS EAGLES SERIES

Just Say Yes ~ Scoring The Player

Playing For Keeps ~ Protecting Her Heart

Against The Boards ~ The First Intermission

The Hardest Shot ~ The Game Changer

Rookie Move ~ The Final Period

Box Set 1 {Books 1-3} ~ Box Set 2 {Books 4-6}

INDIANAPOLIS LIGHTNING SERIES

The Perfect Pitch ~ The Curve Ball

The Screw Ball ~ The Change Up

LYRICS & LOVE SERIES

Marry Me ~ Drunk Girl

Rumor Going 'Round ~ Just A Kiss

STANDALONE TITLES

Tempting Tessa

Until You ~ An Aurora Rose Reynolds Happily Ever Alpha
Crossover Novella

Until Her Smile ~ An Aurora Rose Reynolds Happily Ever
Alpha Crossover Novel

Cocky Doc ~ A Cocky Hero Club Novel

Nothing Bundt Love

SAN FRANCISCO SHOCKWAVES

Ryker

Aiden

ACKNOWLEDGMENTS

To everyone who has supported me, thank you! Thank You for the impact you have made on my life and my writing. Please know that I appreciate you all!

xoxo,

Samantha

ABOUT THE AUTHOR

Samantha Lind is a contemporary romance author. Having spent the first 27 years of her life in Alaska, she now calls Las Vegas home, where she lives with her husband and two sons. She enjoys spending time with her family, traveling, reading, watching hockey (Go Knights Go!), and listening to country music.

Connect with Samantha in the following places:
www.samanthalind.com
samantha@samanthalind.com

Reader Group
Samantha Lind's Alpha Loving Ladies
Good Reads
https://goo.gl/t3R9Vm
Bookbub
https://goo.gl/4XyyLk
Newsletter
https://www.subscribepage.com/SLNL

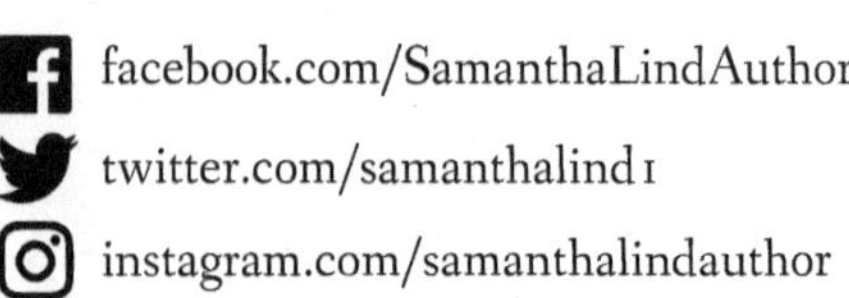

facebook.com/SamanthaLindAuthor
twitter.com/samanthalind1
instagram.com/samanthalindauthor